FORBIDDEN BILLIONAIRE

TS LAYNE

Alphahole Takedown Alert!

"You know what they say, the bigger they are, the harder they fall, and Austin was spectacular at falling."

"Grab your fans and settle in for this racy new series by USA Today Bestselling Author, Tessa Layne, told entirely from the Alphahole's POV"

She was only supposed to be a one-night stand...

Let's face it. I'm a jerk with a big bank account, and that means I call the shots. Until Macey McCaslin. There's only one word to describe the smart, sexy, take-no-prisoners she-devil. *Unforgettable.* And while we may have made an agreement, she's bent on breaking the rules as much as I am.

This may cost me everything, but I'm not staying away...

The only hitch in our little plan? Macey's off-limits. So far off-limits, my brother Jason might kill me if he found out about us. And when he does, because he *will* find out... When I put it all on the line for Macey, the secrets that come tumbling out may break us both.

Chapter One

$\mathcal{N}$o amount of highway driving can erase the taste of Macey McCaslin's pussy from my mind. Not the 101, and not the two days of winding roads that carry me closer and closer to the middle of bumfuck nowhere Kansas and the next ninety days that will be my Purgatory. My indentured servitude to release my trust fund from lockdown.

My Pagani eats roads like this for breakfast, or a shark gobbling up harbor seals. Something I relish as I fly by the speed limit signs, erect in their warning, demanding I slow as I approach Prairie, population 5,672. I accelerate instead, pushing my speed around a particularly sharp curve. I love this car. She may have a fickle Italian engine, but she's a thing of beauty. Curves and lines as luscious and alive as if she's been carved out of Carrara marble instead of metal, leather and fiberglass. She hums beneath me as I press on the gas, purring like a woman begging for more as I fly into the curves. The Flint Hills don't hold a candle to the Pacific Coast Highway, but they'll do for as long as I'm stuck here. I swerve into the oncoming lane and juice the gas to avoid a tractor pulling onto the road.

By the time the speed-limit reads twenty-five, my speedometer reads one-oh-two. A cluster of buildings fly by in a blur, and running the town's only red light gives me a perverse sense of satisfaction. A fuck-you to this whole fucked-up situation. Flashing lights speed toward me in the rearview, and I slow, then pull to the side when I realize I've been tagged.

Of course.

Because my first day in Prairie should read like a Dukes of Hazard rerun. Only the guy walking toward the car looks a lot more menacing than Roscoe P. Coltrane. Funny thing is, I'm not even pissed. I'm bound to find someone as luscious as Daisy Duke hanging around, and I mean to take advantage when I do. Anything to purge Macey from my mind.

I remove my sunglasses and pull my papers from the glove box, holding them out the window with my license. Scary Roscoe takes my papers. "I assume you know you were speeding," he says dryly.

He didn't phrase it as a question, so I remain silent. I catch a glimpse of his nametag: Chief Weston Tucker.

He studies my license, then looks back at me. "I was told to look out for you," he says, handing me back my license and the papers. "I'll let you go with a warning because you're Jason's brother." The way he holds himself makes me think he must be ex-military. There's something about his demeanor that says 'fuck with me and I *will* kill you.' He loops his thumbs over his belt. "But I clock you going anywhere near that speed again and I'll yank your license and impound your car. Got it?"

I give him a salute and replace my sunglasses. "Yes, sir."

Motherfucker. What a fucking day. I pull back onto the road, crawling at what feels like a snail's pace. Ten minutes later, I pull into the dirt drive that's my brother's new home. I shake my head at the somewhat familiar surroundings. They look different with the mid-afternoon sun blazing down. It's been exactly a week since his wedding and I still can't figure out why in the hell he'd give up the easy life to live in this bug-ridden backwater. Clearly his time in the service fucked him up.

I check the dashboard clock. Ten minutes to four. I'm damn well not going to show up early for this meeting. Especially when it's a million degrees outside. I recline my seat and shut my eyes, letting the AC blast over me. The temperature reads ninety-three in the shade. Too fucking hot.

At exactly four o'clock, I shut off the engine and leave my cool haven in search of the tasting room where I'm supposed to 'have a lesson' with Jason's newly hired sommelier. Only this feels more like I've been sent to the headmaster's office for disciplinary action. I might not have the taste buds of a somm, but I was born with a wine-flavored spoon in my mouth, and I sure as hell don't need a 'lesson' from a pretentious asshole with a stick jammed so far up his ass he walks on his tiptoes. I know wine just fine.

Do you? The husky voice that haunts my dreams taunts me.

Yes, I snap back in my head. Somms serve one purpose, and one purpose only, and that's to push wine. They may brag about how refined their palate is, or pontificate about terroir and the fermentation process, and use way too many big words that most people don't understand, but at the end of the day, they're pushers. And if your drug is high-priced wine, then the somm's your supplier.

And the only reason my brother has hired a somm to

run his tasting room way out in the middle of east podunk, is to push wine. Case family wine.

Cougar juice, her voice taunts for the millionth time.

I shake my head, pushing her voice back to the dark recesses of my memory. Macey McCaslin may have been the best fuck of my life, with a pussy that tasted like unicorns and magic, but that ship has sailed.

It's for the best, I tell myself for the umpteenth time. Jason would kill me. Strike that - he'd torture me first, using his super-secret military moves. I like to think he'd start at my toes and work his way up, but I've seen him when he's mad. He'd go straight for my balls and I'd be singing soprano before he cut out my tongue. So yeah, forgetting Macey is the best thing for the family jewels. There's pussy to be had, even in a backwater place like Prairie, and I mean to sample it. Although I may never look at the barreling room on this property the same way again.

My shoes crunch on the gravel, and it's just dusty enough, I know they'll need a polish when I check into the hunting lodge across the road. It's the closest thing to first-class accommodations out here. I push open the door to the tasting room and I'm greeted with a refreshing blast of cool air. Hallefuckinglujah. At least I can get my lesson without drenching my fucking suit.

I pull off my sunglasses and let my eyes adjust to the interior. Half the lights are off, and while I can see a couple of wine bottles and a pair of glasses out, the somm is nowhere in sight. But then I see *her.* She's on the other side of the counter, bent over, but I'd recognize that ass anywhere - whether it's covered in black lace, denim - the way it is now, or my favorite way, bare, creamy, and waiting for my hands. My cock recognizes her too, stiffening at the

Chapter Four

*V*eronica shoots me a glare as I enter the banquet hall where the tasting is taking place. I don't have to look at my watch to know I'm exactly thirty-two minutes late. I timed it that way, heading up to the penthouse suite after I left the bar and pouring myself another bourbon. A little rougher than the Van Winkle 25, but Miles stores my only bottle of that in the safe behind the bar.

Maybe I should have taken a walk, because all I did while I was killing time, was go over every movement the stunning redhead downstairs made. The way her chest rose when she caught me staring. The demure cross of her legs, the strength of her grip on the crystal. The sweep of her lashes when she dropped her gaze. I'm captivated by the memory of her as I stare out over the city. I still hear her voice, ringing in my head like a siren, and if I'm smart, I'll lash myself to the mast like Ulysses, because I'm quite sure if I hear that husky lilt another time, I'll be powerless to walk away.

"Veronica," I murmur, dragging myself back to the

present and giving her a kiss on the cheek the way she likes. Fucking diva, acting like royalty. I don't know how Nico stands it.

She shoots icy daggers at me, the kind that can freeze your balls. "It's about time," she snaps. "Did Nico show you who's on the list?"

"He only just walked up, darling," Nico answers, clearly pissed.

Veronica turns her wrath to Nico. "And if you'd been doing a better job of keeping tabs on your brother this wouldn't have happened."

Declan, my twin, raises an eyebrow and turns his face away before Ronnie can see his smirk. At least I'll have a conspirator tonight. Dec's a little more political than I am. He gives all the fucks I don't, and so far, he's managed to work that to his favor, both with our parents, and in his life. Shit just seems to happen for him. And I'm happy for him. I have no need to be jealous of his success. He's driven in a way I'm not. He clears his throat, turning back to Ronnie. "Calm down, Ronnie. Jason's a sneaky bastard. You can't blame us for not knowing. We took him at his word when he said he was through with the wine industry."

"Will someone explain to me what's going on?" I growl, ready to ditch everyone and head back upstairs. Or better yet, see if Gorgeous Redhead is still hanging around the bar.

Nico thrusts a pamphlet my direction. "Page three."

I flip it open and there, underneath the heading *Moonbeam Acres*, is my half-brother Jason's name listed as associate winemaker. I huff out a laugh, shaking my head. "Dad's gonna shit his pants."

"Ya think?" Declan chuckles.

"Okay, so Dad's gonna freak. But honestly, what's the big deal?" I glance at the pamphlet again. Prairie, Kansas.

"It's not like Kansas is the Napa of the Midwest." Even I know enough about winemaking to know that nothing notable comes from Kansas. "If Jason wants to go play winemaker east of Egypt, what's it to us?"

"The Case family name," Nico grits. "People expect a certain quality when they see our name. He's undermining us."

I snort. "Isn't that going a little far?" There's a reason I prefer beer and spirits to wine. It all tastes like grape-juice to me.

"This is a matter of family honor," he blusters. Beside him, Veronica's red pouty lips pull deeper into a frown. She's had it in for Jason ever since she ditched him for Nico, but as far as I'm concerned, they're all assholes.

I try, but don't quite succeed at not rolling my eyes. I can't believe I gave up *Reservoir Dogs* and a drive along the 101 for this. "Great. So what's the plan?"

"We work our way around the room like we planned," Veronica says.

Of course that's her plan. She wants to see how the other wines stack up against Jason's so she can use that as ammo. Acid rises in the back of my throat. She really is a bitch, and I have half a mind to go find Jason and give him a head's up because once upon a time I worshipped the ground he walked on. But I'm not about to insert myself in the middle of family drama. That would make life anything but headache free.

"I have plans later, so if we're going to taste, let's get going," prods Dec.

Plans, huh? Declan keeps an apartment in the city, and I'd bet even money he's got a plaything in bed anxiously awaiting his return. Maybe two.

I trail after the three, not making any attempt to mask my boredom. Rows of winemakers waiting for a chance to pour their best juice. Hopeful expressions that say they're hoping to be discovered. And I get that. One good write-up, one social media influencer gushing about so-and-so's best kept secret, and their stock could be sold out in less than an hour. I should give lots of shits about this, but I don't.

I smile at a young woman with tits for days and hold out my glass. I should flirt with her, chat her up, but all I can think about is peeling back the black lace dress of a certain redhead. One I'll likely never see again, I remind myself. I should go for the low hanging fruit, but it suddenly seems less appetizing.

We make our way around the room. I hold out my glass for pours from pretty ladies, but to be honest, aside from sweet or dry notes, it all tastes pretty rank to me. I glance down at the pamphlet. Moonbeam Acres is three away. I hang back, wanting to stay above the fray. Nico, Jason and Veronica together in the same room is like a bad chemical spill, and I want to stay as far away from that as possible. Until I catch a glimpse of fiery hair and black lace.

It's her.

Chapter Five

I straighten and push forward. So she was here for the tasting, too? My day just got a helluva lot luckier. But as I approach, Nico, Veronica and Jason are already at it. Their booth is crammed full of people. The man Jason's age looks faintly familiar, but I can't place him. Gorgeous and another blonde, along with an older guy have closed ranks around a third woman with yellow corkscrew curls. There's definitely a standoff going on, but I only have eyes for Gorgeous, and my feet pull me forward as I catch the tail-end of something Jason's saying. "Just being an asshole."

"Who's being an asshole?" I ask, keeping my eyes locked on Gorgeous. Her eyes flash like emeralds as they meet mine.

"Your brother," she spits out in that husky voice that buzzes through me like an electric shock.

That's not a surprise. But before I can process how it is that she's linked me to Nico, I enter full-on flirt mode. I can't help myself. "Well aren't you a sweet, spicy thing?" I shoot back, mouth twitching as I try not to grin. I'm skating on thin ice here, but the way her eyes light as she directs her ire at me says she's ready for a lot more than verbal sparring.

"I don't let my friends swing in the wind," she snaps with a glare.

While I don't have a ferociously loyal bone in my body, Gorgeous here, wears that trait well. So well, arousal pumps through me.

Nico waves at me to join him, then points to the display board. "Take a look at the photos of the vines. I think you'll be surprised by what you see."

I flash Gorgeous my most charming smile. "Excuse me, princess." She carries herself more like a queen, but I'm curious to see how she'll respond. She seems like the kind of woman who'd take offense to that kind of endearment. "I'd love to stay and chat, but duty calls." I smirk and give her a little nod before I move away.

I'm not disappointed. She trails after me as I join Nico who's studying a photo of grape vines. "You don't know the first thing about duty."

I stop and turn, catching her as she collides with me. A jolt of longing rockets straight to my balls. But I know better than to show my cards in front of any of my brothers. They'll pounce on any hint of vulnerability like piranhas. I shake my head with a tsk, letting go of her when she's regained her balance. "I'm surprised, princess. You don't seem like the kind to hand down indictments to people you don't know," I say with a pointed look.

Her cheeks flush and I expect her to back down. I'm pleasantly surprised when she straightens her spine and spears me with a pointed look of her own. "Oh, I know *all* about you."

Feisty little thing. I like her passion, and naturally, my thoughts turn back to a more... pleasurable form of it. Is

I peruse her figure. Slowly. By the time I raise my head, her cheeks have flushed pink. "You're very beautiful, Gorgeous."

Her mouth drops open, and her tongue slicks the center of her lower lip. It's sexy as fuck, and I don't want to be sparring with that mouth, I want to be kissing it, nipping it, coating it with my come. My mouth turns to sawdust as heat rises through me. She extends her hand, and without thinking, I encase elegant long fingers in my own. The shock that races up my arm is powerful, and I involuntarily squeeze. Her eyes widen in surprise as she takes in a sharp breath. Does she feel it too? The heat building between our palms, like a chemical reaction hot enough to melt flesh?

"Macey." Her answer is breathy and heady as moonshine.

"Austin." My mouth curls up. "But I think you already know that."

She nods once, eyes dilated and breath coming shallowly enough I'm aware of the rise and fall of her breasts. I squeeze her hand again, then drop it before I do something stupid like pull her in for a kiss. She reaches for her water, and I shamelessly stare at the column of her throat undulating as she swallows.

Does she realize she's perfection? "Are you hungry? Shall I order you something?" I know I'm an asshole, but I absolutely refuse to eat in front of someone who has no food.

"I spoke with Miles before I sat down. My plate should be out with the wine."

I pounce. "How do you know Miles?"

The corner of her mouth pulls up. Wrong question. I can tell by the look in her eye that she has the upper hand now, and I'm going to have to work for that information. "I've known Miles a long time."

The tone of her voice implies years. Decades, maybe. The man's only forty, and the fact that Miles has history, apparently significant history, with Gorgeous shoots jealous spikes through me. I raise my eyebrows, inviting her to tell me more, but she sits there primly with a Mona Lisa smile.

"If you know Miles, how come I've never seen you here before?"

"I'm only in for a visit."

The mystery surrounding her only deepens. She has a history with Miles, somehow knows my brother, and yet doesn't live here. What am I missing? I'm definitely missing something. "Where *do* you live?"

She lifts a shoulder. "It doesn't matter. What matters is why you're bent on destroying your brother."

And just like that, she's turned the tables again. Frustrating, but I have to admit I admire it. "That's Nico's fight," I say with a wave of my hand.

"And you're just along for the ride." The disgust is evident in her voice, and I don't like how it makes me feel. As if she's disappointed I'm not living up to my potential.

"Jason can do whatever the fuck he wants with his life," I grit. "But he's not going to use us to do it."

"Because that's not what you're doing? Sucking your trust fund dry?"

Damn. So Jason's given her all the dirt? I mean, it's common knowledge in the tabloids that our family is one of the wealthiest in the country, if not the world, but she doesn't seem like the type to waste her time with gossip rags. And it stings that even though we've never met before tonight, I've been weighed in the balance and found wanting. "What I do with my trust fund is none of your damned business, Gorgeous," I snap.

"Jason has every right to use those grapes however he wants." Her eyes sharpen. "Doesn't he? He *is* a Case, after all."

She has a point, but I don't want to give it to her. "Why do you care?"

Chapter Seven

*H*er face softens, and my stomach drops. Fuck me. Is she in love with my brother? Jealousy rises through me like an angry beast. But she leans forward, looking more like a mama bear than a sensuous woman. "Jason is my friend. And after all the pain he's endured, he deserves to keep the happiness he's found."

I won't deny Jason's experienced his share of pain, but clearly my dear brother's been keeping secrets. Before I can manage a witty comeback to that effect, Miles appears with a cart. He lifts a silver dome off the tray, and I'm surprised to see another châteaubriand. How utterly refreshing to dine with a woman who eats more than salad. Without saying a word, he places two wine glasses in front of each of us and impeccably presents the wine. I lift my glass of cabernet. "To discovering beauty in unexpected places."

Macey's cheeks pink and she drops her gaze, taking a sip of the Bordeaux. Her face relaxes as she holds the wine in her mouth, and I catch a glimpse of a wholly sensuous woman who relishes, who savors. I lean in. Watching her like this is the best kind of tortuous foreplay, and I can't help but wonder what else puts this look of ecstasy on her face? When she opens her eyes, they're hazy with pleasure, and my cock is iron in my slacks.

My voice turns to gravel. "What else makes you smile like that, Gorgeous?"

She holds my gaze and the heat builds between us. "You'd love to find out," she finally answers with another Mona Lisa smile.

Fact.

And I'm not about to deny it. "I would."

Heat sizzles in her eyes and the air crackles with unspoken words. But she doesn't take me up on my offer. Instead, she picks up her fork and digs in, cutting a tiny slice of her meat and chewing it thoughtfully before taking another sip of her wine. I'm mildly annoyed she's chosen the French wine over our family's renown reserve cabernet. People waited in line for the '06 vintage. But my irritation is quickly forgotten as I watch her swallow.

Again, the pleasure is evident on her face, and I'm already addicted to it. I don't care if it's pervvy, because let's face it, I'm a total perv. I could get off just watching her eat. Or recreating our own version of the kitchen scene from *9 1/2 Weeks*. I think she knows it, too, because she shoots me a look that's pure triumph. "Your food's getting cold."

"I didn't notice."

Her mouth quirks in amusement and she lifts her glass. "Try a glass? It's a perfect pairing."

I have to ask. "Not the reserve cabernet?"

She studies me and I can tell she's trying to be gentle. "It's not my style," she says after a pause.

"C'mon, you can do better than that," I prod. "Don't hold back."

Her eyes dance with challenge. "Okay, fine. It's cougar juice."

"Cougar juice." I put down my fork and stare at her, incredulous. "*Cougar juice?*"

She lifts a shoulder, her face bland. "It's flabby, over-oaked and too hot."

I grunt.

"And overpriced."

"Tell me more," I snipe sarcastically.

She leans in. "If I'm going to get drunk and have sex, it's going to be with something a little more sophisticated than the equivalent of a frat boy wearing a backward ball cap."

I overlook the dig and lean in so close I can smell her citrusy perfume again. "I like my women sober," I say low enough that only she can hear. "So they know exactly who's making them come apart at the seams."

Her eyes darken. "You're that good, huh?" she answers with a hitch.

I take her bait. Hook, line, and sinker. "Say the word, and you can find out." It would be so easy to move in right now and taste her mouth, taste the fancy wine on her tongue, but she backs away, and the fragile, vulnerable look I remember from our first meeting, flits across her face - as if she's fighting some inner battle. A warning bell jangles in my head, but I'm in too deep, and I'm seeing this game through to the end, whatever its outcome.

"How do I know I can trust you?" she asks.

"I give you my word as... a gentleman."

She huffs out through her nose. "You're no gentleman."

I grin like I'm Mephistopheles offering her most secret desires on a silver platter. "You're right. I'm not worthy enough to lick your sexy little feet, Gorgeous, but pleasure is my crack, not pain."

She rolls her lips together and I can see her mind whirring.

I should sit back and let her come to me, but I want this woman like I want my next breath and I'm not above campaigning. "I promise all you have to do is say the word. You can leave whenever you want, no harm, no foul. And if you think I've done you wrong, go to Jason. He'd love nothing more than to make mincemeat of my face if given the chance."

That seems to satisfy her. She draws a thumb and two fingers up and down the stem of her wine glass, and my cock jumps, because fuck, I want her caressing me like that. She licks her lips and lets out a breath. "I'm okay with touching." Her eyes slant up to catch mine. "All touching, really." Her voice rises at the end as if she's nervous.

Another set of alarm bells jangle, but I'm too close to claiming the brass ring, and she's setting the terms, so I'll go along. "I plan to do far more than touch you, Gorgeous. I plan to fuck you. Hard and repeatedly. But first we start with kissing." I pause to gauge her reaction. Her mouth drops open, eyes turning hungry. "No part of a woman's body should be left unkissed."

"I hope you're a good kisser."

"The best. I'll ruin you for anyone else."

That draws a laugh from her. "Cocky, much?"

I shrug. "I know my strengths."

"We never see each other after tonight?"

Perfect. I pride myself on being the king of first dates. The last time I took a woman to breakfast was the morning of my senior prom, and only because there was a group of us. But she does know my brother and that could be an unpleasant complication. "What about Jason?"

"Only tonight," she states firmly. "And in the very unlikely event that our paths cross again, I'm sure we can both handle it."

I push back from the table and help her with her chair, bending my head to inhale the scent of her. "Done," I murmur into her ear before nipping at her lobe. A shiver ripples across her shoulders before she stands.

I drop my hand to the small of her back, fingers flirting with the curve of her ass. Even touching her there sends sparks of awareness shooting up my arm. Somehow, we manage to exit the bar without seeing Miles. I'm certain he wouldn't approve, but he's not my keeper. Or hers.

"Elevator bay on the left, last one." As soon as the private elevator recognizes my key card and the doors shut us in, I spin and back her against the wall, bracing my hands on either side of her. "Tell me to stop," I say roughly.

Chapter Eight

*S*he responds by pulling on my tie and lifting her mouth to meet mine. "Kiss me," she growls, but in her, it's more like a kitten purring. A chain reaction ignites the second our lips meet. I feel it starting in my head and dominoing through my neck then rushing straight to my balls. I grind my cock into her at the same time my tongue breaches her mouth. I taste the faint remnants of the wine she drank, redolent with oak and fruit, combined with a sweetness that reminds me of strawberries in May, and the tang of arousal. With a groan, I deepen the kiss, wanting to taste more. I never want to taste wine again unless it's on her tongue. Her hands come to my shoulders, and she presses back against my cock, grinding in a way that brings filthy visions of pole dancing into my head.

I hitch up her skirt, searching for skin while we devour each other like it's our last meal. The elevator slides open with a ding, and I realize that was the fastest forty-five-second ride of my life. Somehow, we manage to stumble into the marble foyer without falling.

She drops her hands, surveying my private kingdom. I could live here if I want. At times, I have. To the left is a galley kitchen that opens on one side to the black square dining table set in front of floor to ceiling windows over-looking the bridge. Directly in front and down two steps is a sunken living room with a fireplace and sliding doors to my private balcony. To the right and down a short hall is my master suite.

I'm suddenly filled with the desire to impress her, and it temporarily knocks me off my game, because I'm not sure what impresses her, and I want to know. I come up behind her, trailing my knuckles down the length of her arm. "I can have that whiskey you ordered sent up. Or the Bordeaux."

"I thought you liked your women sober," she teases, giving me a sideways glance.

The back of her dress is open at the top, held together at the neck by a single onyx button, which I slip through, freeing it. The lace falls open, exposing creamy skin and pale gold freckles. I bring my mouth to the base of her neck, tongue tracing a pattern down the top of her spine. "Perhaps this is what you had in mind, then?" I murmur.

Her answer comes out on a hiss. "Yes."

I find the top of her zipper and pull, it slides down her back like a warm knife cutting through butter, all the way to the curve of her ass, barely covered by a thread of lacy thong. I push the dress off her shoulders, and it whispers to the ground, landing around her ankles in a pool of frothy lace. She's a pearl. A Venus rising from the black depths. Dark stockings end in a wide ribbon of lace at her thighs, heightening the contrast between light and dark. I draw a knuckle down her spine, then follow with my mouth. She shivers and twitches, swaying as she lets out a high sigh. I work the clasp at her bra, and she shrugs out of it before turning and displaying herself.

"Someone should paint you," I say, voice thick. Her tits are full and round. In the center, dark peach nipples and areolas are puckered and firm, begging to be sampled. My mouth waters, and I continue my perusal. I see a hint of copper glinting beneath the black lace of her thong, but I'm more captivated by the obviously wet spot at her apex. I step forward and touch the pad of my thumb there, pressing into her softness. She makes a noise deep in her throat and my thumb comes away damp.

If she were anyone else, I'd take her right here. But her body deserves a more thorough exploration. She stares at me unabashedly, eyes glittering, and I step into her space, bringing my hand to the base of her head, and fisting her hair. It's silky and heavy and falls across my hand like a caress. I pull just enough to expose her throat, which I relish with licks and nips, letting the scent of her perfume and arousal fill my brain. She loops her hands around my neck, bringing my mouth to hers in an open kiss, greedily taking my tongue into her mouth. My hands drop to her ass, squeezing and kneading, and somehow, I'm holding her, and we're walking down the hall. She's so wet I can feel it through my shirt.

I set her on the bed and step back, pulling at my tie. "Are you ready, Gorgeous?" I shrug out of my suit jacket and begin to work the buttons of my shirt. "This is the part where I kiss every inch of your body. Starting with your magnificent tits." Her eyes light with a feral hunger that eggs me on. "And then I'm going to rip that flimsy covering off your pussy and spread you wide and taste you."

She hisses in a breath, hips bucking off the bed as she licks her lips. "Then what?" she breathes, eyes lasering in on my cock. I swear it swells under her gaze. "When do I get your cock?"

Fuck. Me.

"You'll get it, Gorgeous. I promise. Where do you want it? Your mouth? Your cunt? I'll fill you up wherever you like."

Her eyes narrow to bright points, and I swear she looks like a tigress, ready to pounce. "Start with my tits." She braces her hands behind her, arching her back so that her tits thrust forward, inviting my touch. I bend over her, mouth hovering over where I know she wants it, and I wait, savoring the anticipation. I lap at her first, bathing the perfect swell in concentric circles, first one and then the other. She groans in frustration. "Please," she utters, arching higher and letting out a sigh of pure satisfaction when I finally take the tight peak into my mouth, rolling my tongue over the point and grazing the skin with my teeth, before sucking hard. Her hand clutches the back of my head, encouraging me, and I take my fill until she's writhing beneath me, every exhale a vocal cue.

My hand drops to the tiny scrap of lace that barely covers her pussy. I snag the elastic and yank. It comes apart with a snap, and I pull on the other side, baring her to me. I push off the bed and take in the neatly trimmed thatch of dark copper. "Open your legs, Gorgeous. Let me see your pretty little pussy."

Her nipples, glistening from the work of my tongue, draw even tighter at my words. God, I love that she likes filthy talk. She's such a contradiction - sweet and sensual on the outside, dirty and wanton on the inside. "I have a name, you know," she sasses, even as she drops her knees wide and exposes swollen pink lips, slick with her arousal.

My mouth waters to taste her. "Do you want me to take you, *Macey*?" Her name catches on my tongue, a foreign, but not unwelcome sensation. "I will take you completely, do you understand?" My voice is rough with desire. "All your pain, your secrets, your past, your longings, your dreams." I pause, letting my words sink in. "All of you. No exceptions." My cock has never ached so painfully. I'm filled with a Berserker kind of lust for this woman spread open before me, like a ripe peach, begging to be devoured. "And then, I'm going to make you come so hard, you forget your name."

Her eyes light as she nods, a slow smile pulling up the corners of her mouth. "Bring it, bad boy."

Chapter Nine

I drop to my knees, spreading her even wider so I can take in the beauty of her pussy, the engorged labia, her bright pink clit poking out like a rose-bud. I place open-mouthed kisses on the silky skin just above where her lacy stockings end, taking my time to taste her, to memorize the musky scent of her arousal.

When I taste her, we both groan. She's a fucking aphrodisiac, a drug, and in that instant, I'm an addict. The sweetness of her hits my tongue first, followed by a spicy, salty finish that I can't get enough of. I could feast on her for days and still be hungry for more. I lick again, more slowly this time, savoring the flavor as it evolves on my tongue. I explore her crevices, memorizing the pattern of her, and where her breath catches. Her hips roll as she seeks more of me and I comply, spreading her wider, and hooking my arms underneath her thighs, pulling her closer. I taste her clit, alternately teasing and sucking, pulling away just before she shatters. "You're killing me," she mutters.

"I promise you won't die."

Chapter Ten

*F*uck. Me.

A four-alarm fire sounds in my head as I stare down at her. What in the fuck just happened? I freeze as I watch a tear squeeze out of her eye and slide down her temple. Fuck. *Fuckfuckfuckfuckfuck.*

I should slap her on the ass and send her on her way. Get as far away from her as possible. I don't do emotions, and I sure as hell don't do tears. It was sex for fuck's sake, not a religious experience. Okay, maybe it *was* a little bit religious. Okay, fine. A lot religious. I forgot my name for chrissakes. But that doesn't change the fact that I need to distance myself and get her out of my penthouse as quickly as possible. I should have known better than to fuck one of Jason's friends. He's gonna slice out my tongue, and then my heart, and then my balls when he finds out about this.

Yet what do I fucking do?

I gather this woman who makes me think dangerous words like *forever* and *infinity* into my arms. I should send her away and pretend like all this never happened. But I don't. I can't, even though that makes me the world's biggest idiot and quite possibly pussy-whipped. I know I'm asking for trouble, but right now I give no shits about anything except soothing her. "Shhh," I say, combing my fingers through her tangled hair. "It's okay baby. Every-thing's gonna be okay." How in the hell do I get her to stop crying?

I sit up and pull her into my lap, running a hand up and down her spine. She burrows into me, clutching my shoulder, sobbing with her whole body. What in the ever-loving fuck is going on? The harder she cries, the more panic builds in my gut. "Did I hurt you sweetheart? Tell me how to help." She shakes her head and cries harder. "What is it?" I feel utterly helpless, and I fucking *hate* it.

"I - I'm okay," she hiccups.

In spite of the lie, a tendril of relief passes through me. At least she's talking. So I continue to hold her, knowing that somehow I'm going to pay for this decision, because I'm going against every instinct in my body telling me to run, and I can't even fucking explain why. I let her cry and cry, while I continue to mumble stupid shit and stroke her back, her arms. I have no clue how long I sit there holding her, but eventually the shaking and the tears subside. I feel like I've just survived a tornado.

"*OhmygodI'msoembarrassed*," she mumbles into my chest when her breathing finally slows. She pushes away, still looking down. "I should go."

"Not so fast, Gorgeous," I say, pulling her back into my lap. "Stay." The words rattle in my mouth, more command than plea, but my chest squeezes at the thought of her walking out of here. "I promised you repeated fucking."

That earns me a laugh, at least, even though it's

Chapter Eleven

*ight weeks later*

MY PULSE QUICKENS as I catch a flash of copper waves through a sea of cowboy hats. It's like a homing beacon in this godforsaken place my half-brother now calls home. In spite of my rules, one night with Gorgeous wasn't nearly enough. For weeks, my heart has stopped every time I've glimpsed red hair. I even went so far as to enter "Macey wine" in the search bar and scour the Moonbeam Acres website for any sign of her. All for nothing.

A throaty laugh floats through the air, the same one that was burned into my ears eight weeks ago alongside filthy visions of naked limbs and eyes glazed with ecstasy. There's no doubt it's her. My skin sizzles with anticipation as my stomach turns in a slow roll, until the sea of cowboys parts and I see who she's with. She's flanked by my brother and his best friend Sterling, the other groom. They're holding onto her and posing for a picture. The heat in my veins turns cold as I look down at the wedding bill someone pressed into my hand, then scan the page again, just to make sure I'm reading it right.

Best Man: Macey McCaslin, standing in for Lt. Johnny McCaslin. You will never be forgotten.

My stomach drops.

I fucked a widow. I've been up nights fantasizing about a gorgeous, sexy widow. Worse? I realize I met Johnny. It was years ago. I was barely thirteen and Jason was a second-year cadet. Sterling and Johnny came home with Jason and proceeded to make my life a living hell for two weeks.

All the unanswered questions I've been mulling over for weeks fall into place with a sickening thud, only to be replaced with new questions. More... emotional questions. I should turn around and get the fuck out of here, Jason's wedding be damned. Everyone knows widows have baggage, and I don't do baggage of any kind. And I certainly don't get into emotional conversations. But I can't stop staring. She's wearing the same dress as last time, and my mouth waters to taste the skin beneath the black lace, trace my tongue along the edge of the thigh-highs I'm sure are underneath.

I scan the page again, just to make sure I'm reading it right, and another name catches my eye. *Flower Girl: Sophie McCaslin.*

Jesus H. Christ. I fucking fucked a MILF. And god help me, I want to do it again.

My mother gives me the stink-eye and motions me to the front row. I stroll up the center aisle, blind to everything except her sensual magnetism that pulls me forward. She looks up, scanning the group, and our eyes lock. My body heats as I hold her gaze, and even though she's a good ten yards away, I can feel the air crackling between us. Her pulse racing every time I see red hair. Restless sleep filled with visions of her face, snippets of our conversations. Jerking off in the shower because vapid socialites no longer interest me. One night with Gorgeous was like the first taste of Pappy Van Winkle I ever tried - it ruined me for other whiskey. "On whether we pick up where we left off."

"We're not picking up anywhere. That night never happened."

"The hickeys I hid for two weeks tell a different story." I drop my head and murmur into her ear. "So do the scratch marks on my back."

Two bright spots blossom on her cheeks, and I want to see that flush make its way to other, more… private parts of her body. She shakes her head, rolling her lower lip underneath her teeth. "You know what I mean." She holds my gaze long enough for me to see the hunger there. "We agreed," she says with a tiny tremble in her voice. "One night only."

"Who says we can't make a new agreement?" I catch another hint of her citrusy perfume and it acts like a spark on a powder keg. Awareness surges through me at the thought of sliding between her thighs one more time, of the scent of her filling my lungs. "If nothing has ever happened between us, then we have a clean slate."

She scans the crowd, and I follow where she's looking - to her daughter laughing up at Jason as he spins her across the dance floor. For an unguarded moment, her face crumples, and I know in that instant, she's thinking of her late husband. The tightness in my chest returns, only to be incinerated by a flash of jealousy so hot, my insides are turned to ash. I wonder, not for the first time today, if he satisfied her the way I did. I push the thought away. I don't care if he did. I'm the one who's here now. I'm the one she's hiding her hunger for now. "I'm flying home tomorrow. You'll never see me again."

"Famous last words."

"I believe they were *your* famous last words, Gorgeous. And I can promise you that I'm never setting foot in this godforsaken place ever again."

Her eyes sharpen. "It's pretty here."

"Pretty remote."

"And the people are nice."

"If you like country bumpkins." I've pissed her off. I can tell by the set of her jaw and the snap in her eyes.

"Has anyone ever told you you're an entitled asshole?"

I grin. "You did, Gorgeous. Right before I gave you your eighth orgasm of the night."

She sucks in a breath, and the blush from her cheeks creeps down her neck. I know exactly what she's thinking of, too. My balls stir at the memory of her spread eagle on my bed, body rosy pink from pleasure, cursing me out as I worked her up to the breaking point, then stopped. I press my advantage. "What would you say if I told you I'm only here because I hoped I might see you again?"

She gives me a pointed stare, voice razor sharp. "I'd say I think you're full of shit. And an asshole," she adds after a pause.

A laugh rumbles through my chest. "I'm definitely that, sweetheart, and your point is?"

Her eyes slide to her daughter, then back to me. She doesn't attempt to hide the hunger on her face. "Twenty minutes. Not a second more, and never again."

Triumph rises through me as I give a silent fist bump. "That's all I need to give you two orgasms."

She rolls her eyes. "How can you live with that level of cockiness?"

"It's confidence, Gorgeous."

She snorts.

"I'm confident I can give you two orgasms in twenty minutes. In fact, I guarandamntee it."

She shakes her head, but I see the smile pulling on the corner of her mouth. "Follow me. You're on the clock starting now."

Chapter Thirteen

*S*he leads me down a path to the other side of the barn. As soon as we're out of sight, I pin her to the wall and claim that sassy mouth. She melts beneath me, one hand tugging on my hair, the other still clutches her tiny bag which scrapes the back of my neck. A moan emanates from deep in her throat.

My thoughts are no longer my own, words tumble out of my mouth without a filter. "Tell me you've been thinking about this as much as I have." I press my cock into her softness. She meets it with a roll of her hips, grinding against me. I'd fuck her right now against the barn if we wouldn't get caught.

"Yes. God, yes," she rasps. "But not here." She pushes me back, then takes my hand. We hurry across the yard to another building. It's nearly dark now, the moon our only light. She pushes on a door and I recognize a crushing room. I stop, pulling her into my arms, but she shakes her head. "In here." Behind her I see another door.

"Barreling room?"

"It locks."

We stumble into the darkness, but that won't do. "Where's the light? I want to see your face again when you come."

Her laugh is low and rich, and she flicks a switch. I blink, seeing her in the harsh light of one yellow bulb. Her face is shadows and planes, but without a doubt there is hunger in her eyes. Need. I take her face between my hands, but this time I kiss her slowly, my tongue moving against hers, tasting the remnants of pink fizzy wine and the heat of desire. I back her against the door, needing to feel her body along my length, wanting all of her. Her bag skitters across the floor. She kisses me back, slow and languid, and my mind spins like I'm wasted. I don't want to rush. I want to take my time, pushing into her sweet pussy over and over again until we're both spent. I want a repeat of the Four Seasons, only this time, I want to wake her up at dawn and take her again. Just so I can see the early morning light play across her face.

"Eighteen minutes," she says breathlessly when we part. She's not wearing a watch, but I get her point. I don't like it, but given we're at a wedding, it's only a matter of time before one of us is missed.

I ruck up her skirt, fingers seeking her silky flesh. She brings a thigh to my hip, allowing me more access, and I slip my hand inside her soaking thong. Fuck, she's so turned on her thighs are slick. My sole focus is claiming that sexy piece of real-estate between her legs.

I drop to my knees, taking her thigh and placing it on my shoulder. Even in the dim light of the barreling room, her pussy is a work of art. Engorged and deep, dusky pink, glistening with her arousal, it begs to be worshipped.

But first, I sink my teeth into the soft flesh just beyond her apex and suck hard, soothing it with my tongue. I want to mark her here, where no one else can see. I want her to remember this when she looks in the mirror. Or touches herself. Her hand grips my hair, tugging so hard that tingles race down the back of my neck.

"Austin," she says through a clenched jaw.

I nuzzle the ligament that attaches her leg to her body. "Mmm-hmm?" I buzz into the flesh, knowing full well the vibrations will reach her clit and drive her wild.

She angles her hips, desperately trying to place her pussy in front of my mouth. "Stop. Teasing."

But I don't give her what she wants. Not yet. "Is your sweet cunt hungry for my mouth?" I make circles with my tongue, almost, but not quite touching her sex.

"You have twelve minutes," she pants, jaw still clenched tight.

Right. I *hate* being on the fucking clock. It makes me all the more determined to make this so intense, she forgets where she is and what time it is. I turn my attention to her other leg, repeating the same teasing motions until she cries out in frustration.

"I swear to god, Austin."

My balls are heavy, my cock thick and straining against my zipper. It's just as angry and wanting as she is.

I turn my face where she wants it, inhaling deeply, taking my fill of her citrusy, musky scent. It's like a drug hit, the way it takes me to another realm. I grip her thighs harder and dive in, taking a long, slow lick from the base of her to her clit, which protrudes hard and needy.

"Again," she rasps, canting her hips.

I oblige because Jesus, it's good. I can't get enough of the taste of her, and if this is the last time for both of us, I want to imprint this into my brain. The salty sweetness of her, the scent of her, the way her pussy fucking glows. She's imprisoned me in some kind of a magic spell that I never want to end. I lick, I thrust, and she shamelessly rides my face, rubbing her pussy against my mouth to get the friction she craves. My cock is painfully hard.

She comes with a cry, back bowing away from the door, thighs going rigid as a shudder rips through her body. With one hand, I manage to remove my belt and drop my pants. My cock springs free and I take a pull to ease the ache. "Condoms," I grate, laying a kiss along her shaking thigh.

"I'm on the pill," she blurts.

I go still.

I risk a look up. Her face is the picture of ecstasy. As long as I live, I won't forget it. Hair wild, dress hitched around her hips, lust burning brightly in her green eyes.

"Are you sure?" I stammer. I don't do bareback. Ever. And yet, it's all I've wanted with Gorgeous from the get-go. My cock jerks in eagerness. *He's* on board with that idea. Completely.

She nods, then bites her lip. "Yes. I want all of you. Just this once."

I pull her thigh from my shoulder and set it at my hip, driving fully into her in one sweet movement. We both grunt in surprise, and then the vixen smiles at me. Because it's that fucking good. The way her wet heat squeezes me makes my breath stick in my throat. Her other leg rises to my hip, and she squeezes her legs together. "Fuck you're good," I utter, my words coming from somewhere other than my brain. My brain is completely occupied with the sensation of her hot pussy encasing my length. I palm her ass, squeezing hard enough I know I may leave marks, and pull out slowly. She bends her head forward with a moan. "How does your pretty cunt like this?"

"Harder."

I think I might die.

But what the lady wants, the lady gets. I thrust harder, slamming into her as she squeezes around me with each thrust. She cants her hips, increasing the friction as I slide through her wetness. I don't know where one of us ends and the other begins. It's only hard pushing into soft, cock into cunt, fingers and teeth into flesh, the ache building to an unbearably sharp point.

"Yes, yes," she chants into my collarbone, biting my neck between words, giving as good as she gets. "I'm coming," she says as her pussy seizes around my cock with such force my vision blurs. "Oh yes, I'm coming."

Her words send me over the edge with her, and I let go with a bellow, pulsing hot jets of my come into the deepest part of her. Over, and over, and over. We still, and in the silence, we hear voices on the other side of the door.

Jesus.

She bites her lip, covering a grin, eyes wide.

I keep thrusting little mini thrusts, and she grinds into me as we shake with repressed laughter. At least the door is locked. The voices on the other side of the door fade, and we both release a deep breath.

With true regret, I place her back on her feet, and smooth her skirt over her hips, then return my clothing to its proper place. Her red lace thong lies on the floor, although I have no memory of how it ended up there. I bend and tuck them into my jacket pocket. "I'm keeping these, Gorgeous."

She rolls her eyes but doesn't object. She smooths her skirt, then bends to retrieve her purse, which she opens, pulling out a lipstick and a tiny mirror. Leaning back against the door, she puts on her lipstick like a pro. Even in the dim light, she looks like a vintage Hollywood movie star. Rita Hayworth, maybe. Nothing out of place except a little extra color in her cheeks to give away her thorough fucking. She rolls her lips together then eyes me, and it's hot as sin. If we were in a movie, this is where she'd ask me for a cigarette. "Let me fly you to San Francisco," I blurt, then immediately wish I hadn't.

Her whole demeanor changes, her body tenses, as does the air between us. She shakes her head and lets out a wry laugh. "I don't do booty calls." She hesitates, and I brace for the blow. "And you're not really my type."

"And what is your type, Gorgeous?" I challenge, offended. With the chemistry we have, I sure as fuck am her type.

She meets my challenge head-on, just like always. "Someone who's honorable. Kindhearted. Dependable."

"I just delivered you two mind-blowing orgasms. On demand," I retort, not willing to admit she's right.

Her head drops back as she laughs, and I'm mesmerized by the undulating column of her throat. When she meets my eyes, I swear there's a hint of sadness there. "You're good for a girl's ego."

She's killing mine, but I'll die before I let on.

She steps forward, and I know this is it - she's the one patting me on the ass and sending me on my way. I don't care for the irony. I brace myself against her scent, now mixed with eau d'sex. She presses a chaste kiss on my cheek and for the briefest of moments, my chest wraps in on itself. But it's gone before the sensation even registers. "Goodbye Austin." She steps back. She takes in a breath like she's going to say more, but instead, shakes her head and slips out the door.

Chapter Fourteen

I make a slow count to thirty, then leave the barreling room without a backward glance. The tables may have been turned on me this time, but I shrug it off. I'm Austin Fucking Case, and when I snap my fingers, the ladies come running. This fling was a blip. A mutually satisfying blip that I will now wash away with another tumblerful of whiskey.

The crowd has thinned, but the hangers-on are just ramping up, and the party has the air of lasting long into the night. Whiskey in hand, I skirt the dance floor. Dec is nowhere to be found, and I wonder if he's seen some action with the blonde bombshell he couldn't keep his eyes off of during the ceremony. A hand lands heavily on my shoulder, and I turn to meet the mottled face of my father. "Where in the hell have you been?" he bellows. I look to my mother, but she won't meet my eyes. The hair on my neck stands up.

"Took a walk."

"You missed the toast," my mother reprimands, with a disappointed look.

I shrug. "Okay. Jase should be glad any of us are here."

"That's no way to talk about your brother," Dad seethes.

What in the royal fuck? "Two days ago you were pissed as hell about all this." I wave a hand around the vineyard. "Why the sudden change of heart?" This is vintage Dad, changing his tune to suit whatever scheme he's cooked up next. It wouldn't surprise me to learn he's un-disowned Jason now that he's married and probably working on babies.

"That's no way to talk to your father," Mom interjects, parroting Dad.

I gulp down half my glass, because if I don't, we'll end up shutting down the party with a shouting match, and while I waste no love on my brother, I don't ever want to be known as *that* asshole - the one that ruined a wedding. Even assholes have standards.

But I can't let it go either. "And what way should I talk to my father, Mom? Should I bend over and kiss his ass the way Nico does? Hoping he'll be named head of the board someday?" I turn and stare down my old man. "Is that what you want? Pops? For me to bend the knee? Make nice with dear old brother?" I know I've crossed the line, even before I see the vein throbbing at his temple. But at the moment, I don't feel like going along with whatever game he's concocted. And I'm no longer a scrawny twelve-year-old he can whip into submission.

"What I *want*," my father starts, clipping each word. "Is for you to take more than a passing interest in the company that has given you everything."

"I know plenty about the business." I might be exaggerating just a bit, but I know enough to bluff my way through the quarterly board meetings I'm required to attend. And I studied business at Stanford for fuck's sake.

It's not like I'm a dumbass who's going to waste money. In fact, he'd probably shit his pants if he knew how much money I've made from investing my trust fund dispersals.

"You don't know the difference between a chardonnay and a cabernet," he blusters.

"Like hell I don't." I can at least tell the difference between white and red. Beyond that? Not so much.

He narrows his eyes. "What are the five grapes of Bordeaux?"

"Does it even matter? All our grapes are grown in the New World." Take that old man.

His eyes bore into me.

"Cabernet sauvignon, cab franc, merlot, malbec, petit verdot," I say in a bored tone. Morrie, our head grower, drilled those into me from the time I could walk. I've forgotten plenty that Morrie told me, but when I was a little kid, I stupidly thought Dad would be proud of me for wanting to know how to make wine. I couldn't have been more wrong. And the fact that suddenly out of nowhere he cares now, makes my blood boil. "Anything else?"

I should have known better than to leave an opening like that for him, because he pounces with the ferocity of a lion. "What's the brix level when we harvest our grapes?"

I have no fucking clue, and from the triumphant look he shoots me, he knows it. He doesn't bother waiting for me to answer.

"What grapes do we use to make Rosé?"

"I don't fucking care," I snap. "It's wine, Dad. We grow it, people buy it. You sent me to Stanford, not wine school."

"And you've squandered your education. On both fronts. Don't think I don't see the way you bluff your way through the board meetings, or the way you spend most of your days doing nothing productive."

He continues on, but I don't hear because my body feels like a million degrees. I feel trapped, cornered, and I don't like where this conversation is headed.

"And I can only hope you've invested some of it wisely, because that's all you have."

"What?" Now he has my attention. "What do you mean?"

"Did you not listen to a word I just said?" he bellows, coming dangerously close to shouting.

My mother lays a hand on his shoulder. "Robert, this isn't good for your heart."

"What's not good for my heart is my three sons sucking our legacy dry. I'll be damned if the Case Family Winery name ends with me." He glares at me. "Let me spell it out, son. I've cut off your access to your trust fund."

"*What?*" I clench the glass in my hand. "You can't do that."

"I can, and I did. And not just yours, Declan's and Nicholas's too."

I nearly laugh, because all I can think of is how that's gonna piss off Ronnie.

"None of you are getting a penny more until you've learned the family business inside and out."

Easy. I was top of my class at Stanford. I can give him a full report inside of a month. But he's still talking.

"And." He holds up a finger. "You've learned from Jason how to make an award-winning wine. It's high time the Case Family regained its reputation for making stellar wines."

There's so much to unpack there, I don't know where to start. "What do you mean 'learn from Jason'?" I ask suspiciously as my brain whirls.

"I mean, you need to get your ass out here next week

after Jason returns from his honeymoon and make me a goddamned winning wine."

I blink, trying and failing to register what he just said. "Are you fucking out of your mind?"

"I'm *fucking* tired of you boys sucking off the family teat and not giving back. I've enacted the kill-clause and your funds are frozen until such time as I deem you worthy."

I've never hated him more than I do right now. Self-righteous asshole, thinking he can still pull the strings and make us dance like marionettes. To make matters worse, Jason appears out of nowhere, looking more relaxed than I've ever seen him. Jeezus, did I enter some kind of parallel universe? Was the whiskey spiked? But as soon as our eyes lock, he scowls. This is the Jason I know and despise. His eyes drop to my knees, then snap back. "Enjoying a bit of the local color, I see?" He glowers at me.

My stomach drops, and I know that my pants must be dusty from the barreling room floor. Fuck. "None of your damned business," I snap, reminding myself I'm no longer twelve and he has no power over me, no matter what bullshit Dad might be trying to pull.

He takes a step closer. "It is when it happens on my property, at *my* wedding."

I'm not intimidated. Not anymore. Not when I'm as tall as he is. "And your point is?"

"Enough, boys," my father orders. "You two can sort this out next week. Austin?" He turns his steely gaze to me. "Don't disappoint me."

Ha. I've disappointed him my whole life. "What if I say no?"

"Your choice. But I wouldn't advise it."

I know what that means. I'll be locked out of everything. Kicked off the estate, persona non grata at the club, hell I wouldn't put it past him to freeze me out of the Four

Seasons. I take a quick inventory of my private investments. I probably have three mil in cash, and another ten to fifteen tied up. I could live off that for a while. Hell, if I wanted to be a beach bum I could live off that the rest of my life. But do I want to? Would it make my life more or less headache-free? It's a toss-up. My life is going to suck dirty balls for the foreseeable future. So the larger question is, do I walk like Jason did? Or do I suck it up because in two years, whether Dad likes it or not, I become fully vested and I can walk away with 2.3 billion dollars in my pocket. The math makes my decision damned easy. And knowing Dad, if I lay low and act like I care until post-harvest, this will all blow over.

"Fine. You win. See you in a week." I don't bother to shake on it or exercise any kind of politeness. I lost this battle, but I'm taking the long view. I'm out to win the war.

Chapter Fifteen

ne week later

"HELLO, GORGEOUS." Clearly, by the look on Macey's face, she's as surprised as I am when I step into the tasting room for my "lesson with the sommelier." I fleetingly wonder why Jason didn't warn her I was coming, but I'm damn sure going to take advantage.

"What are you doing here?" She glares at me. "You promised."

I let the door swing shut behind me, and the sound of the latch catching cuts through the silence. "So I did," I answer with a shrug. "To be honest, you're the last person I expected to see here." I flash her a smile. "But I'm not disappointed."

She shakes her head. "This can't be happening," she says more to herself than me.

"Well, it is, Gorgeous, so I suggest we make the best of it." I can think of half a dozen different ways to begin.

My comment sets something off inside her. "I have a name," she snaps.

"But you are."

Her eyes spark with challenge. "I'm a person. With a name. Fucking use it, or get out of here."

My eyebrows lift. Whoa. Damn if I don't love her fire. But she's right, and if I piss her off, no doubt she'll go running to Jason and I'll have to go live on a beach somewhere in Bali. I open my hands. "I'm sorry… Macey."

She nods, turning back to the bottles behind the counter.

I lean over the counter. "But can I call you that when we fuck?" I tease.

She whips around, shimmering with anger. It's a beautiful sight, and my pulse quickens when she leans in, face inches from mine. I catch a whiff of that citrusy perfume she wears. I swear I will lie on my deathbed remembering her perfume. "We're done fucking, Austin."

She's absolutely right, and I hate it. We can't fuck. Not under my brother's nose. "We should be," I answer, unwilling to completely let go of the idea, to let go of her. And the longer I hold her gaze, the more convinced I become her words are hollow. Her breathing becomes shallow and her lips part. Her face softens and I swear she leans closer.

Neither of us says a word. The silence stretches between us, the air turning heavy with words that should be spoken but won't. I *feel* her wanting me. But I also feel her grim determination to stick to her guns. Awareness hums through my body, my skin tightens, my cells vibrate. I realize with shocking clarity that this enforced Purgatory has turned into hell on earth with Gorgeous working here. I'm not used to this wanting but not having business, and quite frankly, I fucking hate it. I push away from the counter and turn, jamming my hands in my pockets. "Do you know why I'm here?" My voice comes out strangled.

"No."

"My trust fund has been locked up because my father has decided I need to learn to make award-winning wines." I turn at the sound coming from her throat. She's chewing on the inside of her lip, eyes full of amusement. "It's not funny," I bark.

That pushes her into laughter. "Oh yes, it is," she gasps, covering her mouth with a hand.

I glare and try not to think about how beautiful she is when she laughs, when her eyes light up like sparkling jewels.

"So the poor little rich boy has to work for a living," she mocks. "You're right. It's not funny at all." Her eyes narrow. "Have you ever had to work hard for anything in your life?"

"Sure."

"What?"

"My rowing coach worked us to the bone."

"Your rowing coach," she repeats with something like disbelief.

I lift a shoulder. "Yeah. We were a championship team, and that meant long hours in the gym. Miles of running and then rowing."

I realize as I continue to watch her that I've made a serious error in judgment. My answer just confirmed her low opinion of my work life. I start backpedaling. "And I've worked hard on business deals."

"Business deals." She snorts and shakes her head.

Something pulls tight in my chest. I don't like this line of questioning. I don't like the way she's looking at me with something close to disgust. I want her looking at me the way she does when she's coming apart in my hands - like

I'm a fucking god. "I can't help that I was born into a wealthy family," I protest.

She pounces. "But you can help what you've done with that opportunity. Which is nothing."

Her words cut. And I can see by the look on her face, they're meant to. But I refuse to feel guilty about my life choices. I spread my hands. "I'm here, aren't I?" I stalk back to the counter and brace myself. "And let's get one thing straight, Gorgeous." I call her that just because I know it will get a rise, and it does. "Just because I haven't *had* to work, doesn't mean I can't, or I won't. I'll bust my ass for something I want."

"And what do you want, Austin?"

You. But that sure as hell isn't the answer she's looking for. I push off the counter. "I'll know it when I see it."

She makes a disbelieving noise deep in her throat. And for whatever reason - maybe because I'm wound up, maybe because I'm pissed as hell at this bullshit situation - I come right back and pin her with a glare. "Fine. You want me to be honest? I want you, Gorgeous. I want to see your face come undone as you clench around my cock, I want you crying out my name while you're spread open beneath me. I want to taste your beautiful pussy and feel your fingers yanking my hair while you ride my face."

Her mouth drops open as her eyes go round. The air crackles between us. But I know before she says anything, that this time it's not going to go my way. I fight a wave of disappointment.

She clears her throat. "I think if you're here to learn about wine, we should get on with it."

I hold her gaze a moment longer, then nod. "Fine."

. . .

MACEY'S HANDS shake as she sets two glasses on the counter, and I watch her in silence while she sets the space for a tasting. She avoids looking at me, so I study the splash of freckles across her cheeks, still high with color. With deliberate movements, she places six bottles in an arc. An air of confidence blankets her, as if she's done this thousands of times, and again, it makes me curious. What kind of life has she had outside of her friendship with my brother? "How did you end up a somm?"

She flicks a glance my direction. "My parents own a vineyard in the Hudson River Valley."

"That's how you met Jason?" I can just see Jason as a young cadet dragging his buddies to a vineyard just so he could throw his money and knowledge around.

Her face pinches as she nods, and I know she's thinking about her dead husband. Jealousy stabs through me. I have no right. None at all. But I can't help it. And not for the first time, I wonder how on earth the douchebag I remember as Johnny McCaslin wooed and won a woman as beautiful and smart as Macey? And gave her a child? She brushes her hands against her jeans and clears her throat again. "Let's keep the conversation to wine, shall we?"

I *hate* that she's all business again, but I nod. "Where do we start, boss?"

She glances at me sharply, not missing my sarcasm. "We start with you leading the tasting," she shoots back, throwing in a saccharine smile and pushing the first bottle my direction. "I'd hate to insult your intelligence by being redundant."

I push the bottle back her direction. "Maybe I'd like to hear you talk." My mouth curls up. "I'll stop you if it's too easy."

Her mouth bows, pushing out her pink lower lip, and

I'm struck by the color - the same rosy hue as her clit when it's aroused and begging for my touch. I miss her first words, because all I want to do is suck on her lip. Taste it. Hell, taste *her*.

"Are you even listening?" she asks sharply.

"Sorry. Continue." I open my hand to the wine bottles.

She glares at me suspiciously. "As I was saying, I thought we'd start talking about flavor profiles. As a wine-maker, the more you understand what goes into a balanced wine, the better your wine will be."

I don't give a shit about flavor profiles, but I'll play along for the moment. "Great. Hit me."

She opens the first bottle and pours a small amount of pink wine into the bottom of the glasses. "This is your family's cabernet franc rosé from your estate in Napa."

I toss it back managing not to wince as the flavor hits the back of my tongue.

She exhales heavily. "You're supposed to smell it first. Observe it. Then taste it." She refills the bottom of my glass. "What do you notice?"

Nothing that she wants me to notice, and everything she doesn't. Like the way her hair glows when the sunlight catches it. I make a show of swirling my glass and taking a big sniff. Nothing. I don't smell a goddamned thing. And I know there's nothing wrong with my nose because I sure as hell can smell her perfume. "What's going on here?" I ask a little too sharply.

She shoots me a knowing smile. "The wine's too cold, masking the aromas of bright fruit. But this is how most people drink it."

"And your point is?"

"The winemaker created a wine so bold that it cuts through the cold. The problem only comes when you drink the wine at fifty-five degrees or higher."

"Let me guess," I start with a wry smile. "Over-oaked, flabby and hot?"

She gives me her Mona Lisa smile as she pours another rosé into the bottom of the next glass. It fizzes, and I recognize the label from my brother's wine. I take a sip. The bubbles explode on my tongue in a manner that hints at arousal. Foreplay. It's sensuous and effervescent, and when the taste of strawberries hits my tongue, all I can think of is how I want to pour this over Macey's pussy, then slowly lick it off.

My cock likes that visual a lot. Too much. My mouth turns to dust, and I down the rest of the glass in a gulp. Macey clucks her disappointment, but I'm done with this lesson. "So what's the point? There's got to be more to it than one is Stellaluna, and the other's from my family's vineyard."

Her eyebrows rocket and a smile pulls at the corners of her mouth. "Stellaluna?"

"Isn't that what you call it?" I give her a look I'm sure conveys my impatience. "You're going to tell me it's all cougar juice, right?"

She covers her mouth, hiding a smile and shaking her head.

"What?" I growl. "What's so funny?" I'm half a second away from getting in the car and driving back to California. Family fortune be damned.

"It's called Stardust Rosé, and we don't make cougar juice here."

"Fine. Whatever. I still don't see what the purpose is."

"Stellaluna is a children's story about a bat."

Definitely not cougar juice.

"Sophie has it. You should ask her to read it to you sometime."

"Thanks, I'll pass." The last thing I want is to hang out

with a little kid reading a story about a bat, even if she's adorable and looks just like her mother.

Her eyes flash with something I can't quite identify, and just like that, her face is all business again. "The point is, hot stuff, it's the same grape. It's the winemaker that makes something special," she snaps. "And if you bothered to learn anything about your family's business, you'd already know that. You want to get out of here and go back to your fancy life in California? Figure out how to make something classier than cougar juice."

I lean over the counter, done with this bullshit and her air of superiority. "That's why I'm here, Gorgeous." My words come out clipped. "And you can be *damned* sure I'm going to take good notes and get out of this hell-hole as soon as I fucking can. Tell my brother when he's ready to play winemaker, he can find me at the hunting lodge."

Chapter Sixteen

I cool my heels two days before Jason finally shows up, face like a thunderstorm. "Where in the hell have you been?"

"Right here where I told your sommelier I'd be. Where have *you* been?" This is vintage Jason, and this time, I'm not falling for it. "I showed up right on time, just like the dutiful son I am, and was subjected to a humiliating lesson in wine quality-"

"Which you would already be aware of if you paid any attention at all instead of focusing on your next lay."

"I haven't been laid in weeks," I bristle. Okay, it's been about ten days, but it was weeks before that. Gorgeous has ruined me for other pussy.

"And you won't be, because I swear I will rip your balls off if you make a pass at anyone while you're here."

"Who died and made you my keeper?" My hand twitches. I don't like fighting. I think it's a waste of time, but Jason makes me want to punch something. Every. Single. Time.

I swear, he grows six inches taller as we stare each other

down. "Dad. And I have strict instructions to send you packing at the first sign of trouble."

"Since when are you and Dad back on speaking terms?"

"Since I made a deal with him about keeping our vines," he acknowledges. "But that doesn't mean I trust him or like him any more than the rest of you."

I grind my molars. Right now, I hate all of them. But Jason has severely underestimated my desire to keep my trust fund if he thinks I'm going to fold that quickly. I can bend the knee for ninety days if it means I'm free of all of them after that. And if I can convince Macey to give in to her baser desires during that time, even better. One more taste of her is all the motivation I need to go through three months of hell. "You can tell Dad I'm a motherfucking angel, then."

Jason's mouth quirks. We may not like each other, but we're Cases. Unified in our dislike of the old man and the way he manipulates us. "We'll see about that. In the meantime, get your ass out to the vineyard."

"You're kidding."

Jason's eyes turn hard. "Like fuck I am."

"It's a million degrees outside."

"Tough shit. You need to understand pruning."

"I understand it just fine. That's what the internet is for."

"I don't give a shit what the interwebz might have told you about pruning, you're going to see it for yourself, now get your ass across the road in thirty minutes or you can go the fuck home."

"Fuck you, asshole," I growl, all pretense of playing nice lost. Jason can kiss my fucking ass.

"Thirty minutes," he growls back, and turns on his heel. He has me over a fucking barrel and he knows it. But

I'm not showing up a second before thirty minutes has passed, and maybe even a few minutes late, just to spite him. I'm going to have the last laugh though, when I walk out of here a free man.

Thirty-five minutes later, I meet my brother at the edge of the vineyard. It's not even ten a.m., and I've sweat through my shirt. Jason takes one look at my clothing and rolls his eyes. "Let's get to work." He turns and hikes down a row of vines, not bothering to see if I follow, which I don't.

"Did you expect overalls?" I call after him. Nobody told me I was supposed to bring farmer clothes with me. I don't even own farmer clothes, but whatever. My Armani loafers are leather, just like the boots Jason now prefers. And my Givenchy jeans may caress my thighs like one of Macey's kisses, but it's still denim. "Ninety days," I mutter to myself. "I can stand on my head for ninety days." I'm going to be so fucking good at standing on my head, I should take up yoga. And nothing says I can't look good doing it.

I catch up with him, and he points to a vine, laden with fruit. "You said you studied up, hotshot? What's wrong with this vine?"

I refrain from rolling my eyes. The fastest way to get him off my back is to play along. "Too much fruit."

"And what fruit do you cut away?"

"Depends." I swallow the stream of profanity I'd prefer to let out. One of the reasons I was co-captain of the men's rowing team at Stanford was because I was always cool under pressure. It may be Jason pushing my buttons right now, and he does it better than most, but he's not getting the upper hand. Not today, not ever.

"On what?"

I can hear in his voice he expects me to fuck this up,

but I used my two days of waiting wisely. There's not much he'll be able to surprise me with today. "On the size of the shoot for starters," I say in a monotone. "How many clusters each shoot has, and whether or not the shoots and clusters are too close together."

He makes a noise in his throat. I've surprised him, at least. Maybe even impressed him. But he's not done trying to trip me up. "What do you recommend here?"

"You're the winemaker, not me."

He glares at me, and the silence stretches between us. I've put him in a tight spot, and he knows it. If I give him an unsatisfactory answer, he'll claim he's the winemaker and he knows best. But if he suggests that I am, and I'm *right*, then he loses his leverage, and he knows it. After an uncomfortable moment, he clears his throat. "Hypothetically speaking, *if* you were the winemaker, what would you do?"

"Not grow grapes here, for starters."

That earns me a darker glare. "Say you lived here," he clips out.

I smirk, and I know that makes me an asshole, but I can't help it. "I'd eliminate any fruit on a short shoot. On shoots eighteen to twenty-five, maybe twenty-six inches, I'd allow one cluster, and only two on anything bigger. Unless the clusters are too close, then I'd go to one, and allow extra space between the clusters since it's humid here."

He grunts and studies the ground, then hands me a pair of pruners. "Then get to work." He stalks off without another word, the scrape of his prosthetic hitting the dirt, the only sound except for a bird chattering in the distance.

Again, I swallow a stream of profanity. It's not worth fighting him now. We'll have our reckoning when I have more leverage. Inside of an hour, I'm dripping and I've already popped a blister, but I'll be damned if I reach for a pair of gloves. I pull off my shirt and hang it on the hedge. This is shit work, and I hate every second of it. And I can't for the life of me fathom why my brother insists on doing this work himself. Craft beer is so much easier. So is distillation, for that matter. "No wonder Case Family Wines makes so much cougar juice," I grumble. "The ROI is so much better."

"Better than what?" Macey's husky voice calls out immediately behind me.

I whirl, dropping my pruners. "Jesus Christ, woman. Didn't anyone tell you not to sneak up on someone when they're holding sharp objects?"

Her laughter dies as she peruses my sweat slicked chest. I crick my neck and roll a shoulder, flexing my pecs. Only because my muscles are screaming at me. "I- I thought you might be thirsty," she holds out a thermos. "It's lemonade. With basil." I raise an eyebrow, and she rushes on, using all her breath. "And I thought you could use some sunscreen. It can be brutal out here."

"You don't say."

She's wearing a sundress today, pale pink cotton the color of which makes me think indecent thoughts, and a flush begins just above her pert, round breasts and travels up across her collarbone, along the column of her neck, and into her cheeks. She looks as luscious and ripe as the first summer strawberry. And god help me, but I want a fucking taste. Fancy basil lemonade won't begin to quench the thirst I have for her. "There are water stations at the end of each row, Gorgeous," I drawl, pinning her with a stare. "Why are you really here?"

Chapter Seventeen

*M*acey's eyes drift down to the bulge in my groin. Her face transforms from merely curious, to hungry, and I love the undisguised desire I see there.

My voice drops an octave. "Careful, Gorgeous. Keep looking at me like that and I'll bury myself so deep in that pretty little cunt of yours, you won't know which way is up."

A slow smile cuts across the lines of her face, and she licks her lips, slow and hungry, as if she's the one who's going to be doing the devouring. "Really?" she asks, voice husky and eager.

My cock strains against my jeans. It's uncivilized, how much I want the woman before me. She brings out the primal caveman in me. I'm used to being in control, carefully orchestrating every interaction to my satisfaction, and more importantly, my quick exit. But this fiery redhead with the wide smile and the eyes that flash dark promise has me reeling, spinning out of orbit. It's unsettling, but more than that, it's deeply erotic. It calls to a part of me I didn't know existed. A part of me that runs on pure instinct and a need to possess. Wholly.

She steps forward, placing a hand along my length, and lets out an appreciative hum as she strokes me like there are no barriers between us, and we have all the time in the world.

"I mean it, Gorgeous," I growl. "Ever heard the phrase *don't poke the bear?*"

She answers by giving me a squeeze. "What about the bear... poking?" Then she drags a finger down my sternum, not stopping until it rests on the button of my jeans.

Fucking tease, sent to torture me by some angry god I've displeased. I should send her away and put us both out of our misery. I draw strength from some unknown source deep down and tamp down the heat boiling in my veins. "Don't you have a tasting room to run?" I ask with a cough.

She gives me her Mona Lisa smile. "Only Thursday through Sunday."

Jeezus, between the Kansas heat, and the fire she's stoking in my veins, I'm going to have a stroke out here. "Your kid," I ask with a note of desperation. "Where's your kid?" I'm grasping at straws, but I know if I give in I'll be lost, or worse, Jason will catch us in flagrante. And then I'll be dead. Literally.

"*Sophie's* at day camp," she pointedly uses her daughter's name, but I have no intention of playing Uncle Austin while I'm stuck here. She hikes up her the edge of her dress, exposing a creamy, satiny length of thigh. "I can't stop thinking about what you said in the tasting room." She takes my hand and pulls it under her skirt. Fucking hell, she's not wearing panties. And she's shaved, or waxed, or something, because her pussy is as smooth and soft as the finest silk satin.

Fuck. Me.

I'm a goner, and the cat-ate-the-canary expression on Macey's face says she knows it, too. "Are you trying to kill me?" I grit. For once in my life, I really am trying to be a goddamned gentleman.

She wiggles against my fingers. "I can't sleep at night," she breathes. "Because all I can think about is your mouth on me. Your cock inside me."

That's it. I can't fucking stand it another second. I clasp her sex, letting her arousal slick my palm while I fist my hand in her thick waves and pull down. I give her one breath to protest or change her mind and then I claim her. I devour her mouth with all the pent-up energy I've been storing for days, stroking her tongue into submission, bending her to my body. I'm breathing hard when I come up for air. "Is this what you want, Gorgeous? Is this what you've been dreaming of?"

"Yes," she answers on a moan, clutching the tops of my arms.

I want her so badly, I'm nearly blind with it. But some primitive, danger-detecting part of my monkey brain sends a current of warning through me. The hair on my neck stands up, and I tear my mouth from hers and push her back, letting her skirt fall back to her knees.

"What in the-" the rest of her words are stifled, along with the glare I know she sent my direction.

I bend, bracing my hands on my thighs, trying to re-order the contents of my brain and catch my breath before my brother reaches us.

"Everything okay?" he asks tersely, once he's within earshot.

"I... ah... I think he's had a little too much sun." Macey manages to sound mildly concerned, all trace of desire wiped from her voice.

"Jesus, fuck," grits Jason. "How much water have you had?"

"Enough," I spit out before I return to standing.

He looks at me sharply. "You're bright red."

He knows.

An instant of stomach dropping terror overtakes me, but I make sure it passes. Everyone knows the best defense is a good offense. "No shit, Sherlock. It's a million fucking degrees outside."

"This isn't California, dumbass."

"Really?" I don't even try to disguise my sarcasm. "A rash guard wasn't on my packing list."

"Macey, can you help him get back to the lodge? He's done enough."

"I hope my work was satisfactory," I grumble. I can tell by his lack of comeback it was, and I know that irks him.

"I want you back out here tomorrow at the ass-crack of dawn," he calls after me. "And for fuck's sake, go into town and buy some proper clothing."

"You really do look like you need something to drink," she says when Jason's out of earshot.

I need a helluva lot more than something to drink, starting with an ice bath. I glare at her. "That's all you can say when my brother nearly caught us with my fingers up your pussy?"

"You don't have to be so crass about it." She bends to pick up the thermos, face flushing.

"And you don't have to pretend you're offended," I snap back, crossing my arms. "You like those words just fine when my tongue's down your throat, or my fingers or my cock is inside you. Or when you're telling me exactly what you want," I add with a pointed arch of my brows.

Her eyes flash, and she opens her mouth to protest but

shuts it just as quickly when I pin her with a look that dares her to disagree.

"So what will it be, Gorgeous?" I know we're both rattled by the near miss with Jason, and while the caveman in me wants to take her right here, I can sense an air of panic settling over her. "Are we scratching that itch that's making you so hot and bothered, or are we forgetting this ever happened?"

Her eyes lock onto mine and I fight a wave of disappointment at what I see. I reach for my shirt and shrug it on, wincing at how it sticks to my sweat-slicked torso. I refuse to beg. "You know where to find me," I toss over my shoulder as I walk away.

"Austin, wait," she calls after me, even though she makes no move to catch up.

I keep walking, reminding myself of all the reasons that Macey McCaslin is bad news, and ignoring the tightness in my chest that says otherwise.

Chapter Eighteen

*C*ockblocked.

Nothing says cockblocked quite like three-hundred-thirty-six hours of backbreaking labor and spontaneous check-ins by my keeper. Not that I'm counting. At first, I was convinced Jason had our number. Six times in the last two weeks he turned up completely unexpectedly, and while I may have been standing too close to one captivating redhead, my hands were in plain sight. The worst time was when he showed up with Sophie, making it very clear who the man in her life was. Not that I care. I don't want to be anyone's man. I just want to release the agony coiled up in my balls. It's so bad, I think my dick might fall off. And to be quite honest, I can't go on like this. Something has to give.

I have another 'lesson' today with Gorgeous. I've been alternating days in the vineyard with lessons about each of the grapes our family grows. And after everything I've learned, I want to fire the entire goddamned board. Whose idea was it to diversify so profoundly? It's bullshit and a waste of resources, and if I haven't been kicked off the board by the time I get back to Napa, I'm going to have a thing or two to say about it. I'm burning to ask Jason a few questions on the subject, but hell if I'm going to let him think I might actually care about what's going on with the business. I'd ruin my reputation as a dilettante if I did that.

I step into the tasting room and let my eyes adjust, bracing myself for my body's inevitable response to the woman I can't seem to purge from my system. My blood feels heavy in my veins, pulsing a slow thrum of anticipation.

She waits at the counter primly wrapped in white linen and cotton, like a librarian on summer vacation. And because I'm a dirty pervert, I immediately wonder what's underneath her wide-legged pants, and whether or not her pussy will feel like silk when I touch it. My mouth turns to sawdust, but somehow I manage to rasp "Hello, Gorgeous." I let the door swing shut behind me. She doesn't even look up this time.

This is the way it's gone for two weeks now. First with cabernet sauvignon, then with cab franc and pinot noir, followed by syrah, merlot, and grenache. And we haven't even started on the whites. I always make a point of poking the bear, and most times receive a glare in return. Next I try shameless flirting, which always induces a pretty stain on her cheeks, but never anything more. Once, I caught her staring at me with such naked desire, I nearly jizzed my shorts right there. Sadly, this is our dance. But now I'm sick of it.

Six bottles of sangiovese stand ready to pour. She's covered the labels, so I have no idea which one comes from our family's holdings. "What can you tell me about sangiovese?" she asks while scribbling notes onto a stack of three-by-fives.

"Not even a hello, how are you?" I tease.

She rolls her eyes and keeps writing.

"What if I'd injured myself working in the vineyard yesterday?"

She snorts.

"Well?"

"I'm sure Jason would have taken you to the clinic," she says dryly.

I brace myself on the counter. "You missed me, didn't you?"

She tries not to smile, but I see the twitch at the corner of her mouth. Damn if I don't want to kiss the plump little dimple.

"Sangiovese," she repeats severely. "Now."

I'm sick of the quizzes, of the assumptions that still persist after two weeks of showing everyone here I know what I'm doing. I've studied. I've studied more than they realize. It didn't take me long to figure out where we're hemorrhaging money. They should let me have my trust fund for that realization alone. But no, I have to pretend I give a shit about the rest of the business. All it's made me want to do is open a distillery. "Fine. Sangiovese is the most planted grape in Italy, grown primarily in Tuscany, but as far south as Sicily," I rattle off with a bored tone. "It's the primary component in Chianti, and also Brunello di Montalcino."

That earns me the look of approval I've been craving. "You've been studying," she says, obviously impressed.

I preen, standing taller, leaning closer. "You don't know the half of it."

But she's a hard nut to crack, and she turns back to her cards. "Flavor profiles."

"Medium-bodied, notes of cherry, strawberries, and pepper. It likes oak and takes on notes of leather and tobacco when aged." She raises her brows as she digests my recitation, but I'm not done. "It thrives in shitty soil and is prone to overgrowth in rich soil. It's drought-tolerant and needs a longer growing season. It responds well to malolactic fermentation in new oak, taking on notes of vanilla."

The smile she gifts me with goes straight to my toes. Have words like *malolactic*, and *tannins* become a new form of foreplay? Does it make her wet when I say *Montalcino*? My fingers itch to discover. "You could be a somm, you know, if you weren't so stubborn."

I ignore the needle. "I don't give a fuck about wine, Bridge," I say, quoting a line from Bridget Jones I overheard her mentioning to Jason's wife Millie a week earlier. "Tell me about kissing girls in boarding school."

She covers a laugh and shakes her head, but her eyes are sparkling. "What about when it's grown in California?"

I've been waiting for that question. She's asked the same questions for each varietal. "Notes of cherry are present no matter where it's grown. But it suffers in Napa's rich soil, becoming flabby and flat."

"Where does your family grow Sangiovese?"

I'm ready for that question too. "Dry Creek Valley. And the eastern Columbia River Valley."

And a small amount, so small I don't even count it, in Napa. But I should have, because she pounces.

"What about in Napa?"

"That's less than a hundred barrels."

"Still, it's a vineyard your family owns."

"Pour the wine," I growl. My next challenge will be to decide which wine is the one made by Case Family Wineries. If it's anything like the previous tastings, the worst one will be from my family, something that irritates the shit out of me. And I'm starting to see her point about our wines having no nuance, and generally being too big, like the overweight asshole at Thanksgiving, or the middle manager at a company party that bloviates with a voice so loud it can be heard in the restroom.

She pours into two glasses. She always tastes too, which I love, because it's the only time I get to see the expression of pure appreciation on her face. It's riveting, and I might wack off to it late at night when I can't sleep. Someday, I'm going to put that expression on her face. Until then, I have to satisfy myself with glimpses of it when we taste.

I swirl the first glass, then sniff, just like I was taught. Sangiovese isn't very aromatic. Not compared to cab franc or cab sauvignon, but I do catch a hint of cherry, and a note of oak. I take a sip, shutting my eyes to fully concentrate on the flavors passing over my tongue. There's fruit, and roundness, and leather. And I think of smoke fired pizza, roasted tomatoes and fresh mozzarella baked to a golden crisp. This has to be Italian. But all thoughts leave my brain when I open my eyes and I lock gazes with Gorgeous, who looks like she wants to eat me for dinner.

And I want that, too.

I try and reach for adjectives, descriptors I've rehearsed, but I'm hypnotized by her expression and the way her eyes narrow into glowing gems of promise. She's a cobra and I'm her prey, and I'm powerless to stop the words that tumble out of my mouth. "I want to see you again, Macey."

My heart pounds with the admission. I've never said those words. They're not in my vocabulary, and certainly not how I roll where women are concerned. But I think I have to admit I'm an addict. The first step to recovery is admission, right?

She sips in a deep breath and pushes away from the counter, turning her back to me. Her answer comes out strangled. "You can't."

"Why not?"

"It should be obvious by now."

It is, and the obstacles are real. "But I know you feel what's between us. Why deny it?" I press. "Why deny yourself?"

She turns back with a glare. "It doesn't matter what I feel, or what I want. What matters is that I have responsibilities, other people to think about." She shakes her head. "It's too risky."

And in that moment, another piece of the Macey puzzle drops into place. I stalk around the countertop, stopping only when we're toe to toe. "That's it, isn't it? You've always denied yourself, haven't you?"

She drops her gaze.

A tongue of protective anger spools through my belly. I wonder what kind of man she married that demanded that kind of sacrifice from her. If she was mine, I'd spoil her rotten from sunup to sundown. But I push those dangerous thoughts aside. "When have you ever put yourself first?" I already know the answer. She's not prone to abandon, and yet it suits her magnificently.

I crook a finger under her chin, giving a gentle tug, and pull her gaze up.

Her eyes search mine, but she doesn't answer.

I press on because I can't stop. Not while there's a chance for something more. Not until we've reached some kind of closure. "It scares you, doesn't it? The power you feel when you let go?"

She worries her bottom lip.

I pick her up and seat her on the bar, stepping between her thighs. "Macey," I say, voice dropping an octave. "Don't run away from this. There's so much pleasure to be had. You deserve it," I croon. "All of it." She sways forward, eyes half-lidded. I want to kiss her, devour her.

Take her on the bar, but I hold back. "You call all the shots. No emotions, just sex."

"Just sex," she murmurs back.

"I promise, we'll be discreet."

"No one can find out," she murmurs, hand coming to my bicep.

"It will be our secret." I bring a hand to the base of her head, caressing the knot of muscles at her neck. "We just need to fuck until we've fucked each other right out of our systems."

A shudder wracks her. "Yeah," she breathes out with a nod. "That." Her voice comes out squeezed.

"I'm going to kiss you now, Macey. And then I'm going to lock the tasting room doors and fuck you on the counter. You okay with that?"

"Yes." She nods, eyes dark with hunger. She squeezes her legs to my hips and pulls me in for a kiss. Our mouths meet in a collision of tongues and lips, and my cock strains against my zipper.

We stay locked together until the sound of our heavy breathing bounces off the limestone walls of the tasting room. She breaks the kiss and waves a hand behind her. "Door," she says in a breathless rush. "Now."

Chapter Nineteen

I jog across the room, pulling at my shirttails. I've waited too damned long for this moment. Behind me, I register the soft clinking of wine bottles being shoved aside. The scrape of glass on the concrete countertop acts like a fingernail trailing down my spine. My body tenses at the unspoken promise crackling in the air. It's only been a few weeks, but it feels like a lifetime.

The deadbolt settles into place with a loud *snick*, and I turn, making my way back to where she's laid herself out on the countertop like a pinup girl. "Don't move a muscle," I order gruffly, crossing the space in three long strides. She's kicked off her shoes, and I start by taking her ankle and pulling her dainty foot to my mouth. I press a kiss on the arch, a movement as intimate as it is erotic, because I've already memorized every nook and cranny of her body. She sucks in a breath and stares down at me through half-wild eyes filled with expectation. I repeat the motion a little higher, pushing the wide pant leg past her knee. We have more than twenty minutes this time, and I mean to take full advantage. We have the place to ourselves - Jason's across town, helping on the ranch where his veteran buddies live, and his wife and her father have gone to Manhattan.

"Is your pussy already wet for me?"

Her thighs tighten and she bites down on her lower lip. "So wet," she answers brokenly on an inbreath.

"Show me."

Her hands fly to the buttons at her waist. Hips rise and shimmy. In seconds, she's bare to me, and it's the most beautiful thing I've seen since I arrived at this godforsaken place. Her light fuzz of copper glows in the light streaming through the window like some kind of a pussy halo. She never ceases to surprise. She's like Christmas morning and birthdays wrapped into one. And whether it's bushy or bare, it's all delicious holiday candy to me.

Beneath, I can see her pussy wet and slick with the evidence of her arousal, the lips swollen and dark pink, curling out like a beautiful, edible flower. I'm struck by the memory of a Georgia O'Keefe painting I saw at a museum gala once, and how her pussy blossoms under my stare. My mouth waters to taste her. But not yet - not until she's laid out before me like a feast. Still, I can't resist a little touch. I draw a finger up the inside of her thigh, marveling at the goosebumps that arise in its wake. Her curls are soft against my knuckle

"You're stunning," I say, not recognizing my own voice.

Her hands fidget, first spreading then fisting on the countertop, then trailing over her hips. I still them with my own, bringing her fingers to my lips, tasting each delicate tip in turn. By the time I'm finished, she's panting and pulling at the buttons on the simple oxford shirt that hides her curves. Again, I pause. I love the unwrapping, the slow reveal that drives my imagination wild, the hint of skin exposed when the fabric, released from its bondage, falls away in a deep vee. I catch a glimpse of pale pink lace, creamy skin, and golden freckles. It doesn't matter that I've memorized the taste and feel of her, I still get a thrill when her shirt slides off and miles of creamy skin is brought to light, because there is nothing more sublime than the female body in repose, soft curves pink with eager expectation, waiting to be worshipped. And worship her, I will.

The fabric drops from her shoulders with a sigh, pooling behind her on the counter. Sheer pink lace is the only remaining barrier, covering the lush, pale swell of perfectly shaped breasts, punctuated with a rosy orb in the center, pushing mightily against the material. My breath stills in my throat as I take in the sight before me. From here until forever, I will never see anything but her when I'm in this room, the way the sunlight bounces off her hair, the golden light playing across her belly, the pearlescent quality of her skin, luminous against the industrial gray countertop.

I loom over her, shadowing her body with my own, and drop my head. The citrusy scent of her rises from the valley between her breasts, filling my head with rainbow colored sparks, as light and effervescent as champagne bubbles. I cover her nipple with my mouth, the fabric rough against my tongue. With a needy moan, she arches into me, an unspoken plea for more. I snap the front clasp and push away the straps. Her breasts rise and fall with her shallow breaths, and I swipe my knuckles along the underswell, hungry for the sensation of her satin skin against mine.

My cock is like iron, aching and weeping against my belly, the engorged head painfully restrained by my waistband. Lust thrums in my veins, heating my blood to boiling. I drop my shirt to the floor and our gazes lock. Hers, dark and hungry, I'm sure, mirroring my own. With a purr, she raises her arms above her head, colliding with a bottle and sending it flying. I don't know how I manage to catch it before it lands, but I do, splashing the contents across her belly in the process. The bright red wine paints her skin like a Jackson Pollack painting, glinting like rubies. A stray droplet catches my eye as it wanders down her hipbone, pulled by gravity to the juncture of hip and thigh, until it disappears in the crevice next to her pussy. I draw open her legs and chase the red path left by the bead of wine with my tongue. It's exquisite, the taste of her mingled with the fruity tang of sangiovese. I lap up every drop until her belly is washed clean. I growl low in my throat, a signal of my appreciation, before I settle myself between her legs and finish with a long, slow swipe of her pussy, a heady compliment to the flavors swirling in my mouth, and one I must taste again and again.

But just to be sure, because we've been down this road before, I lift my head and wait for her to meet my eyes. With a gasp, she lifts her head. I half expect to see glittering emerald points, and a razor sharp remark to fall off her tongue, but there's a softness in the way she contemplates me that pulls dangerously at my chest, that speaks of words neither of us want to speak or hear. "Just sex, right, Gorgeous?" I remind her, my heart hammering near my throat.

She gives the barest nod. "Nothing more," she says with a throaty whisper. "What are you waiting for?"

Chapter Twenty

What am I waiting for? I grin with the impish delight of a devil. "Everything, Gorgeous. I want your full surrender."

My comment earns me one of her wickedly amused smiles that makes my cock jump. She rolls her hips, and the invitation is one I will never in a million years, pass up. I nip the sensitive flesh of her thigh hard enough to mark her, then caress the spot with my tongue, working my way back to the part of her I love most.

She lets out a long low moan as I feast on her. The sound is music to my ears, and I slow my movements, lapping up her arousal with the languid thoroughness of a cat grooming in the sun. "Ohh yes," she whispers raggedly, more to herself than me, but I know she's close when her fingers fist in my hair. The pain spikes across my scalp and runs straight to my cock. I seal my mouth around her clit, and glance up. Her head is arched back, mouth open wide, body undulating as she rockets toward a shuddering climax. This is better than any five-star dessert or thousand dollar whiskey. I growl in appreciation as she bucks and shakes, a sheen of sweat popping across her chest, and I let her rock against my mouth until her body goes limp.

I push up from the counter. "Hang on, Gorgeous. That was just the first course."

She gives me a wicked smile, eyes bright and radiating satisfaction.

"I have condoms," I offer, reaching into my pocket, but she shakes her head.

"Not unless you prefer." Her voice trails off at the end.

"Are you fucking kidding me? Your pussy is heaven without a condom." I toe off my shoes and drop my pants. "Heaven." My belt clatters on the floor, the perfect punctuation to my comment.

She rolls to her side, propping her head in her hand, and peruses my body, eyes landing on my cock. It thickens under her heated gaze, bobbing and jerking, begging to be petted. Her mouth tips up and she purrs as she reaches out, tracing my engorged head with the pad of a finger. Her touch is electric, sending a white hot shock down my shaft.

"Fuck, Macey," I grunt.

"Yes, please," she answers, fingers flicking down my shaft to play with my balls. "I want it hard, big guy, will you fuck me hard?"

JesusfuckmytittiesifIhadthemChrist. With a growl that sounds more animal than human, I climb onto the counter and push her onto her back. I pull her thigh up, and she hooks a calf around my ass as I slide balls deep with a single powerful thrust. She responds with a gasp then a sigh. Her nails dig into my shoulders but I feel no pain. How could I when my cock is ensconced in tight, wet, heat? I thrust hard again, just so I can hear the noise that comes from her throat, and once again, dangerous thoughts enter my head. Forever thoughts. The kind of thoughts that have no place in a 'no strings attached let's fuck each other out of our systems' agreement. She meets my thrusts with squeezes of her own, and the heat between us melts my skin. We're molten elements, flesh and bone fusing in a timeless chemical interaction that drives us higher and higher. I. Can't. Get. Enough.

With each thrust we climb higher and higher. The energy coils at the base of my spine, poised to rocket us both into the stratosphere. When she comes, it's with a loud series of cries, each one pitched higher than the other, and she convulses around me, squeezing my cock with a rippling motion that blinds me with the pleasure of it. I groan too, when my orgasm hits with the force of a wildebeest stampeding down a ravine. I thrust once, twice, three times, emptying myself into her with animal like ferocity. I dimly register the sound of breaking glass, but that could be my head exploding for all I know, because we've fucked ourselves onto another plane of existence.

Our breath comes in deep shuddering sighs as reality slowly creeps back into our awareness. I press a kiss to her temple, not quite ready to relinquish the moment. "I think we broke the bottles," she says, voice wry with amusement.

"I'll pay for new ones."

"Money can't fix everything."

"I gaurandamntee you it can replace every single bottle we broke. Just text me the list, I'll have Miles get on it right away."

Her gaze flicks back to mine. "Miles?" Her voice is weighted with surprise, but also amusement. I feel like I'm missing something, but I can't quite put my finger on it. At least not in my present state.

"Sure. Why not? That's what he's there for."

"I'm sure he has nothing more important to do." I don't miss the sarcasm in her voice.

"It's his job, Gorgeous. It's what he gets paid to do." I can feel the tension building between us again, and I pull out, then push off the counter. I don't care to argue buck naked in a tasting room. She follows suit, and for the next few minutes, the only sound in the room is the brush of clothing against skin, zippers being pulled, shoes slipped on. I'm pissed now, more at the loss of my post-orgasmic buzz than at our next round of sparring. Still, it jangles.

"Shoot, I have to run," she says apologetically, phone in hand. "I have to pick Sophie up at day camp. Can you take care of the bottles?" She waves a hand at the floor.

I blink.

She's dismissed me. I can't believe she's just dismissed me. Patted me on the ass and sent me on my way. I fucking hate it. But I agreed to let her call the shots, I remind myself. What kind of magic did she weave that for three seconds I was mister nice guy? Fuck me. "When will I see you again?"

She gives me the Mona Lisa smile. I'm coming to hate that smile, what it means - because it means her mask is firmly in place, and more and more I want the real Macey. "I'll text you." She pulls a hair band out of her pants pocket and in a fluid motion, pulls her hair up into a messy bun, the kind of bun I'd love to run my fingers through. But before I can stop her, or kiss her, or even ask how in the hell she already has my number, she's crossed the room, unlocked the door, and slipped out without a backward glance.

Chapter Twenty-One

*T*he text comes four hours, twenty-six minutes, and fourteen seconds later. Not that I was counting.

M: *835 W. 11ᵗʰ*

My jaw swings open as I stare at the address. I've never been on the receiving end of a booty call, but clearly, that's what it is. I have half a mind to ignore it, but my cock has other ideas. I wait five minutes before typing a reply.

A: *I assume this is where you live?*

M: :)

Unfuckingbelievable. I briefly consider walking across the hall and showing this to Declan, but I'm fairly sure he's sexting with the blonde with the corkscrew curls from the wedding. Dec's been in this godforsaken backwater almost as long as I've been here. We're staying across the hall from each other, yet we've been like ships passing in the night. I'm sure Jason orchestrated it that way, but I also know for a fact that Declan has spent a total of two nights here since we arrived. Although calling them nights is a stretch. I bet he hasn't even unpacked his suitcase.

But instead of giving Dec the third degree, I take a quick shower and shave. Two can play the waiting game, and just to be sure, I want her to know unequivocally that I don't come at the snap of a finger. Even for her. I step out quietly into the twilight, the night air warm and humid against my skin. Fireflies wink across the yard as I slip into my Pagani. I pull apart the little aluminum miniature of my car to expose the key, then pause, fingers hovering at the ignition in the center console. She's not subtle, my girl. As soon as I fire her up, everyone within a quarter mile will know I'm headed out. Just so long as that intel doesn't make its way back to Jason. But pussy is calling, and who am I to turn down *that* invitation? Especially when it's been extended by a woman whose pussy tastes as exquisite as hers?

I turn the key and the car roars to life beneath me, and I feel the vibrations deep in my sac. By the time I arrive at the bungalow on West Eleventh, I'm ready for a full night of lovin'. Only Macey has other ideas.

"What are you doing here?" she hisses, looking over her shoulder when she answers the door, and stepping onto the porch, pulling the door partially shut behind her. Clearly she has no intention of letting me inside.

"What do you mean? You told me to come over."

She makes a face. "Not in that." She points to my baby.

I turn my head to take in the one thing that's as beautiful as the woman in front of me. "Uhh…. that's my car. Should I have Ubered?" Can you even call an Uber in a town this small?

"Oh god no." She shakes her head with a look of horror. "Everyone in town would know what was up inside of an hour."

"So," I spread my hands. "I should have walked?"

"You should have come in something more discreet."

"More discreet." I know I sound like an idiot, repeating her words, but to be honest, I'm dumbfounded. "You should have given me clearer instructions."

Her eyes go wide. "I did."

I scoff. "The last time I checked, smiley face emojis were not explicit instructions."

"Let me see your phone." She sticks out her hand.

"For real?"

She nods. "Hurry up. Mrs. Townsend is staring out the window."

"Who?"

She stands on tiptoe, craning her neck to peer over my shoulder, clearly ill at ease. "Mrs. Townsend, across the street. She doesn't miss a thing. And if your car is here any longer than five more minutes, it's *still* going to be all over town first thing in the morning. Everyone knows your car."

"How do you figure?"

She rolls her eyes. "How many people have one of those… " She flicks her fingers in the direction of my car.

"Pagani?" I supply.

"I've never even heard of that."

"It's Italian."

"My point is, it sticks out like a sore thumb. Everyone in town knows you're the man with the weird car."

"That car," I protest, pointing back at my baby, "is a work of art. Not. Weird."

"Okay, whatever." She gestures toward me again. "Show me your phone."

I hand it over, and she gasps, pressing a hand to her pale cheek. "I knew this was a bad idea."

"No it's not." I state flatly.

"Look." She offers her phone.

Sure enough, there was a follow-up message she sent,

telling me to park in the alley behind her house. But the text still hasn't shown up on my phone. Fucking dead-zones. "Shit. I'm sorry."

She waves, presumably at Mrs. Townsend. I turn and wave too, only to see the curtains fluttering. "You have to go," she says, placing a hand firmly on my chest.

"Should I park around back?" I'm not ready to give up on this, and if I have to park across town and sneak back like a delinquent teenager, my cock and I are both on board with that.

She lets out a sigh. "I think it's a bad idea. It's like she has bionic hearing *and* x-ray vision."

"Maybe you should move," I offer wryly.

"Unh-unh," she says emphatically, shaking her head. "Not with the park and the school within walking distance. "Are you kidding?"

I guess I was.

"Mommy?" a high voice drifts forward from the back of the house.

Macey grimaces. "I'll be right there," she calls over her shoulder. She turns back, chagrined. "I'm so sorry. Another time."

Before I can even pull her into my arms for a good-night kiss, she's shut the door, leaving me alone on the porch.

Frustration boils up through me, but there's nothing I can do when I've been cockblocked by a nosy neighbor and a five-year-old. With regret, I turn and hop down the steps, waving at the old biddy who I'm sure is lurking behind the curtains. Once I'm inside my car, I give her the finger and rev the gas extra hard as the engine fires up.

Chapter Twenty-Two

*M*y next summons comes six days later.

Is this a booty call? I text back.

A few minutes later, her reply: *I don't do booty calls.*

"Like hell you don't," I say with a laugh. I can picture her as she typed it - spine straight, expression conveying a sense of superiority. At her instigation, we've managed to sneak fucks in about every nook and cranny throughout the vineyard, but this time I'm ready. I pull up to the front of the house in my brand new Dodge 2500 pickup. It's been an adjustment, switching to a vehicle so slow to respond to the gas and sluggish on the turns. But as long as I fit in with the local color and neither Mrs. Townsend or my brother suspect anything, then I'd drive a Dodge Dart if it would help me spend the night with Macey.

I reach across the seat to grab the bottle of Midleton Bluebell that arrived, special order, the other day. I've been waiting for the right moment to give it to her.

She meets me on the porch, eyes wide with surprise. "What is this?"

I flick my eyebrows high with a grin. "Just a little something I thought you'd like."

She covers her mouth with a hand, shoulders shaking. She's hiding an amused smile, and it knocks me off-kilter, like I've made an error in judgment. "I don't get it," she says, eyes darting from the truck back to me. "It's not really your style."

And then it hits me. She means the truck. I cover my disappointment with a shrug. "Of course it's not," I rumble, placing the whiskey on the wide stone rail that's more like a bench, and closing the distance between us and coming to where she leans against one of the stone pillars holding up the roof. She's wearing cutoff shorts, loosely slung at her hips. The denim is soft and worn and my fingers ache to skim it, to slip under the fringe to the soft places beneath. I push her hair back from her shoulder and lean in for a kiss, but she stiffens. "What? What is it?" She points her eyes in the direction of the house across the street. Fucking Mrs. Townsend must be at the window again. I step back, jamming my hands in my pockets.

"Why'd you buy it?" she asks when I'm standing a respectable distance away.

"Why do you think, Gorgeous?"

She looks at me oddly, a mixture of surprise and appreciation, and it makes my chest tight. "You'd be noticeable no matter what you drove, Austin. Some people were meant to stand out." It's the closest thing to a real compliment she's ever offered, aside from the obvious comments about how great my cock is. Which it is. But this is different, and I'm surprised by the admiration in her voice. I can tell she means it, and my insides warm at her words. I clear my throat and drop my gaze. Her feet are bare, nails freshly painted in a shade of pink that makes me think of her tits when they're aroused. Women in my world only have bare feet in the bedroom, and the fact that she's talking with me in bare feet implies a level of intimacy, of familiarity I'm not comfortable with at all. Like she trusts me. And I am definitely not trustworthy. At least not in matters of the heart.

I need to steer things back to safe territory. And by safe, I mean fucking. No doe-eyes or anything smacking of emotional crap. I need to regain control of whatever it is we're doing because it's not a fucking relationship. I may have told her she could call the shots, but that stops today. "I should go, I just wanted to bring that by." I gesture to the bottle.

"This?" She picks it up, then shoots me a sharp glance as realization dawns. "You brought me this? How did you…" her voice trails off as her eyes move in a triangle from me to the truck to the bottle she holds.

"Not many people appreciate that kind of quality."

"Thank you," she says, voice going breathy.

I hate the way her voice works its way through my body, pulling at me, calling me closer. But tonight I'm not giving in. I lift a shoulder. "It was nothing," I lie. "A friend came across it, and I remembered you like it."

She tilts her head sideways, assessing me. "Sophie's asleep." Her voice takes on a seductive quality that turns my cock to steel. "Come in for a sip?"

I give a silent fist pump. I'm back in control of this game. "Better not if neighbor lady is watching."

Her eyes dart behind me, and I feel a strange sense of relief at her look of disappointment. "You're right," she says with a sigh. "Next time, maybe you should walk."

"From across town?" I say with more than a little incredulity. I shake my head, a little of my old swagger coming back. "I don't think so, Gorgeous."

"Then park your car, or your truck, or whatever you're

going to drive next at the park, or the school, or-or, somewhere."

"Why?" I tease the back of my finger along her jaw. "Is that sweet cunt of yours hungry again? Such a greedy thing," I tease.

A shiver runs through her body, but she shakes her head. "I think Jason heard us yesterday."

"Why? What happened?" I ask sharply. I'll be damned if I let him take away the only good thing that's come out of my enforced servitude.

"He asked me to keep an eye on the crushing pad door, and to remind the day hands that the crushing pad and barreling room are off-limits."

My stomach lurches. We snuck into the barreling room at lunch yesterday, and I'd made her come loud and long. But we thought everyone had gone into town. I clench my jaw and give a nod. "Maybe we need to cool it, then." My cock might protest, but we're skating on thin ice, and I need to get a fucking grip.

Our resolve doesn't even last twenty-four hours.

I don't know if that makes me the world's greatest fool, or the world's smartest man. Because, pussy. Macey's pussy, specifically, which seems to have put me under a spell. Only unlike Ulysses, I haven't lashed myself to the mast. I've indulged, over and over and over, and it may be the end of me.

Chapter Twenty-Three

*J*ason bursts into the tasting room where I'm bent over my laptop, studying the spreadsheet of yet another vineyard my family owns that's not living up to its potential. This place is barely breaking even and they should be bringing in three times that. At least. They're growing pinot noir in the Russian River Valley for fuck's sake.

"I need you to drive over to Macey's," he says gruffly.

My head snaps up, and I'm immediately on guard. "Why?"

"We've got a private party booked this afternoon and she's got childcare issues."

"Why can't she bring Sophie here?" It's not like Sophie hasn't been here before. She runs around like she owns the place on weekends.

Jason scowls. "Does everything have to be a battle with you?"

I snap my laptop shut. "I'm pretty sure the family business doesn't include babysitting."

"It does when my somm has a childcare emergency

and I need her here an hour ago," he bristles, irritation sparking off him.

"Then tell me what the emergency is," I grit out.

"None of your damn business," he yells.

"Like hell it isn't," I yell back. It always goes this way. Ever since... well, since ever. But I'll be damned if I'm going to be relegated to babysitter.

Jason glares at me, eyes glowing embers. "Here's the deal, and if word gets out, I'll know exactly where it came from."

That grabs my attention. I'm all ears.

Jason takes a deep breath, and for a fleeting moment looks... anxious. I'm too surprised by the look on his face to listen and I miss the first part of what he says.

"What?"

"I *said*, Millie's pregnant." He looks at me expectantly, as if he expects me to start jumping around and clapping or something.

"Okay."

That earns me another glare. "That's all you have to say? Okay?"

"What do you want me to say?" I snap.

"Congratulations might be nice."

If I cared, which I don't. "Your life, your choice."

"You're a fucking asshat."

"Look who I learned it from."

He rolls his eyes. "Okay, I deserved that."

He deserves so much more than that, and it's all I can do to not take advantage of this information and bring up the years of shit hanging between us. But it won't accomplish anything, and the sooner I get out of here and back to my old life, the better off I'll be.

The edge comes off Jason's voice. "I wouldn't ask you if there was anyone else."

"Thanks for the vote of confidence," I say with as much sarcasm as I can muster.

He sighs heavily and runs a hand through his close-cropped hair. Even after retirement, he's still chosen to keep his hair regulation short. "Look, I know you don't like kids, but Sophie's great."

"I wouldn't know, the way you and Sterling fuss at her like two mother hens."

"Yeah, well it's our job. We made a promise to Macey."

That's news to me. Although to be fair, I've been so busy mining Macey's pussy, I haven't asked much about Sophie. She seems nice enough as far as kids go, but I have no desire to stick my nose or my person where it doesn't belong, and Jason and Sterling have made it clear I don't belong anywhere near Sophie. "So why can't Sterling watch her?"

He grimaces. "Emma's pregnant, too," he says after a pause.

"And I care about this, why?" I open my hands in question.

"Because two kids at the day camp came down with Rubella, and they've had to shut it down."

"Okay?" I don't even know what the fuck Rubella is.

Jason looks at me like I'm an idiot.

"If you want my help, don't look at me like I'm a fucking moron."

"It's a form of measles that causes birth defects in unborn children."

Oh. But wait a minute… "So you want *me* to go hang out with a kid who's been exposed to *measles*?" Unfucking-believable. No. Fucking believable. I shake my head firmly. "No. Fucking. Way."

Jason looks like he's warring with himself. "Please? I'd owe you one."

I drop my head back with a laugh. A long, deep belly laugh. "Say that one more time?"

Jason glowers at me with open dislike, and I fucking love it. He *hates* that he's had to come to me and I plan to use this to my advantage. My brain whirls, because an opportunity like this won't present itself again, and I need to capitalize on it. Wring as much concession from him as I can. If I was Jacob and he was Esau, I'd ask for his birthright, but I don't want what Jason has. I want freedom, and only unlocking my trust fund will give me that. "Help me make a rosé as good as the one you made."

Jason's eyes widen. "Come again?"

"You heard me. Help me make a rosé as good as the one you made."

His eyes narrow. "Why should I help you?"

"Why should I help you?" I reach for my laptop bag. I get all the way to the door before he calls out.

"Are you willing to do exactly what I tell you?"

My hand rests on the knob. He knows doing what he says won't be easy - there's too much baggage between us, too much resentment. I don't love my brother. I don't even like him. But I'd be a fool to underestimate him. I'm confident he won't undermine me - he wants me gone as much as I do. I go over the numbers again in my head. I could be a beach bum for the rest of my life with the money I currently have. But it's not enough. Not after going over the conglomerate's numbers with a fine-toothed comb. We're flabby and bloated, just like our wines. And I could make it better. *I want to make it better.*

The realization hits me like an anvil. My rowing coach's words ring in my head. *Nobody likes a half-assed loser. Go down fighting or get out of my boat.* I rowed my balls off for Coach Mickey. Everyone did. He inspired us to row even when we had nothing left in the tank. No one in my family inspires me, and I don't give a shit what they think of me. But I do give a shit about what Coach Mickey would say if he saw me half-ass an opportunity to win big. I turn around and eye my brother. I'm going to hate every second of this, but I'll do it. Because I'm not walking away a half-assed loser. "Yeah. I am."

Chapter Twenty-Four

*M*y truck rolls to a stop in front of Mrs. Townsend's house, and I make a point of waving when I get out. She can let the whole town know I'm here for all I care. I'll get hero points when Jason confirms I'm doing him a solid.

Macey answers the door with a guilty smile. "Thank you so much for doing this, we all appreciate it."

We all. The fact that I'm an outsider in the Macey-Jason-Sterling besties triangle grates at me. I know Macey's body inside and out - the super sensitive spots that drive her wild when I kiss them, the way she likes her oral, and just how hard she likes her gorgeous nipples sucked. I know she loves to make out while we're fucking, but only if we're not in a hurry. I know she likes variety. I know her in all the ways that matter to keep her pleasured... and nothing else. And suddenly, I like that a whole lot less.

I can't ask about her past, because all roads point to Johnny McCaslin and his ghost that stands between us. And I sure as fuck can't ask about her future, because this is just a fling. Nothing more. But now that I've been made the adult in charge of her daughter, it doesn't feel right that I know nothing more about her than she's a somm, and she likes to quote Bridget Jones on occasion.

"Austin?" Her brows knit together. "Are you okay?"

"Yeah, yeah." I nod, giving myself a mental shake. This is just business, I remind myself. I don't want to be on the inside. There's too much baggage to deal with, too much emotion.

Her face melts into an expression of relief. "Good, good. Sophie's just finishing up breakfast. Why don't you come in and say hi." She steps back and lets me into the house. I step cautiously into the inner sanctum I've been trying to breach for weeks, suddenly ill at ease. The irony that I'm here at my brother's invitation, and to do no more than babysit, isn't lost on me. It's modest, but tidy. The wood floors and fixtures look to be original. Macey leads me into the kitchen, where her mini-me sits at the table. "Soph, you remember Uncle Jason's brother, Austin?"

She turns her big blue eyes on me, and fuck me, it's like she can see straight into my soul. "You're the one Uncle Jason doesn't like."

"*Sophie*," Macey admonishes, cheeks burning bright.

I wave her off. "It's okay." It's awkward as fuck, but I'll manage.

"No, it's not," Macey answers firmly, staring directly at Sophie. "She needs to remember her manners."

"Why doesn't Uncle Jason like you?"

I jump in before Macey can respond. "Because big brothers never like their little brothers."

Sophie gives me an assessing look, then nods. "Joey doesn't like his little brother. He says he's a brat."

"Sophie." Macey's voice holds a note of warning.

"Most little brothers are," I say, relieved that my answer was enough.

"Can you please take your cereal bowl to the dishwasher?" Macey asks Sophie.

Sophie scoots off the chair and carries her dish to the sink, where she climbs on a stool, rinses it, then places it in the dishwasher. I'm slack-jawed as I watch. I've never seen anything like it. Macey turns to me. "Sophie can help you make sandwiches at lunch. You can go to the park this morning. The kids at day camp usually lay down after lunch. I told Sophie she could watch a movie or read books. I'll be home by dinner time."

"We'll be fine." Inside, I'm less certain. I don't know the first thing about kids - what they like, what they don't like, and most importantly, how to keep them safe. As soon as Macey leaves, I'll be consulting the hive mind called Google.

Macey bends to give Sophie a hug, and when the little girl's chubby arms wrap around her mother's, and I see the fierce love reflected in Macey's face, my chest squeezes tight. The pain is so sharp I have to look away. I look back just in time to see Macy placing a kiss on her daughter's forehead, and then she turns to me. "Are you sure you're up for this?"

"Yep," I lie. I'm absolutely not up for this, but I'll manage. Compared to lashings and cigarette burns in the barn, this will be a cakewalk.

Only it isn't.

Sophie is an insane monster, and I swear she's powered by atomic energy. It's freaky how smart she is, and the kid is fearless. I mean, *fear-less*. I step into the bathroom to take a piss and come out to her doing backflips on the couch. "*Sophie,*" I say sharply, rushing to where she is. "I'm pretty sure you're not allowed to do that."

"Yes, I am," she says primly with a challenging smile. "Ask my mom."

She's a fucking little devil and she knows I'm not going to bother Macey. "How about dolls. You have dolls, don't you?"

She scowls. "Dolls are for sissies."

I have to remind myself this is the daughter of an Army Ranger, and both her 'uncles', are retired Rangers. They probably taught her to swing from trees before she could walk. "Okay…" I stretch out the last syllable, at a loss for what to suggest next. "Books?"

She crosses her arms. "Park."

"Park, okay. We can go to the park." Then I realize Macey didn't leave me a key. I get the feeling that if I say no to the park I'm going to be dealing with hellfire and brimstone. I hold up a finger. "Hang on a sec, I need to ask your mom where the key is."

"We don't lock the door," she says matter-of-factly, staring me down with her enormous blue eyes.

"Of course, you do. Everyone locks their door when they leave the house."

"We don't."

"I'm sure you do, sweetheart. Let me just ask your mom." I shoot off a quick text. *You forgot to tell me where the key is?*

She texts right back. *Don't worry about locking it, you'll be fine.*

A: *Seriously?*

M: *Yes.*

I can't fucking believe it. Who - in this day and age - leaves their door unlocked?!? Jeezus. Does she leave it unlocked at night, too? Visions of all kinds of vicious and violent outcomes fill my head. I swear to God, if I have to camp outside her house every night from here on out because she won't lock her damned door, I'll do it. *We're talking about this later,* I text back before jamming my phone in my pocket. "All right, kiddo. I guess we're going to the park." Sophie shoots me a smile of pure 'I told you so' and flounces out the door, ruffly skirt bouncing with her.

"Hey, wait," I call after her. "You forgot your shoes." But she's already grabbed the bike I saw lying in the grass and is pedaling down the street hell for leather, red curls flying behind her. I grab the pair of pink and purple sneakers by the front door. Motherfucker. Then I notice the helmet on the front step. I grab that too as I jog after the little hellion, cursing Jason with each out breath. This has to be his doing. Surely Macey isn't the type of parent who lets her daughter run wild?

My leather soles slip on the gravel as I cross the intersection. I manage to catch myself before I fall spread-eagle. "Macey," I holler. "I mean Sophie. *STOP.*" But she's too far ahead. I swear I will wring her neck when I reach her. Visions of her falling and breaking an arm, or being hit by a car, fly through my mind with alarming vividness. Macey will kill me if anything happens to her. Hell, I might kill myself. I'm winded and sweaty when I finally reach her. She's dumped her bike at the edge of the playground and has climbed to the very top of the jungle gym. "Sophie," I bellow. "Get your ass down here. *NOW.*"

She looks down at me, eyes snapping, just like her mother. "I'm telling mommy you said a bad word."

"And I'm telling mommy you rode to the park in bare feet without your helmet." I hold up the evidence of her disobedience.

Her eyes narrow.

I narrow mine back.

If this were a Clint Eastwood movie, both our hands would be twitching above our six-shooters.

In the end, she decides to climb down, and I breathe a sigh of relief. I check my watch. It's only ten-thirty.

I am so screwed.

Chapter Twenty-Five

*B*y the time Macey arrives home, I'm exhausted. Wiped. Out. And ready to call the doctor for a fucking vasectomy. It must show on my face because she gives me a look of sympathy as she drops her purse by the door. "Oh you poor thing."

I glare at her.

"I'm sorry. I should have warned you. Sophie can be…" she searches for a word. Six come to mind, none of them polite, or anything you would tell a mother. "A handful."

"Indeed." Honestly, I'm grateful the kid didn't die on my watch. And that I didn't kill her, because on at least four occasions, I was ready to string her up by her toes. Cuteness be damned.

"Stay for dinner?"

Tempting, but no. I shake my head. "Sorry." She looks so crestfallen, I nearly change my mind. But I need a break from Wild Child. "How about later?" As in, long after she's asleep.

Now, Macey shakes her head. "Mrs. Townsend."

"I'll walk from the park."

"What if you park in the alley?"

"Won't other people see?"

"I don't think the other neighbors are as interested as Mrs. Townsend."

I study her, taking my time as I scan her figure, prettily attired in the pale pink dress I like so much. She stares back, eyes hungry. I feel the same way. It's been days since we've been able to sneak a fuck, and the idea of laying her down between soft sheets brings my cock to life with a jolt. "Nine p.m.?"

"Ten."

I nod. "Will the door be locked?"

"I'll leave it open."

"If you do, I may have to spank you."

Her eyes light. "Promise?"

It's so tempting, but her safety is more important. "Keep it locked, Macey," I growl. "There are assholes and criminals out there. Even in small towns."

She lets out a sigh. "Fine. I wouldn't want you to worry, or anything," She adds with an eye roll.

Quick as lightning I rise from the couch and capture her wrist, pulling her flush against me. "I will always worry about your gorgeous little ass."

It was meant to be more playful than it came out, and the air between us grows heavy. Her breathing becomes more shallow, and I can see her pulse pounding at the hollow of her neck. My mouth waters to taste her, but it's too risky. If Sophie-the-hell-child saw us kissing, it would be game over. I'd be dead. I force myself to step back. "Until ten."

"Until ten," she echoes, barely above a whisper.

THE PUNGENT SMELL of a Cuban cigar hits my nose when I reach the lodge.

Declan.

I follow my nose around the corner of the building to find Dec wearing a light colored linen suit and lounging in an Adirondack chair. He's got a cigar in one hand and a tumbler filled with ice cubes and whiskey in the other.

"That better not be my Pappy Van Winkle you're polluting with ice cubes," I say as I drop into the chair next to him.

"Sadly, no." He motions to the paper bag beside the chair.

I grab it and pull out the bottle. Johnny Walker Blue. "Man, you're slumming it."

Dec gives me a wry smile. "It was the best bottle they had at the liquor store."

"So why the celebration?" If he's enjoying whiskey and a cigar before midnight, something's definitely up.

"Just added to my real-estate empire today."

"Congratulations." I take a swig straight out of the bottle since there's no other glass to be had. And fuck if I haven't earned it today.

Dec puffs out a halo of blue smoke. "Ask me where."

"Bahamas," I guess. Dec's been savvier with his trust fund disbursements than I have, and has built quite a name for himself in real estate circles. He'll be better off than me if he ditched his trust fund, which is why I haven't been able to figure out why he consented to this whole stupid "learn to make wine, or else" arrangement. He likes wine even less than I do.

"Guess again."

"Grand Cayman."

"Farther north."

I'm too damned tired to be playing this game. I take another swig from the bottle. "Quit fucking with me."

He side-eyes me and swirls the ice in his glass. "You hear from Nico today?"

I hardly ever hear from Nico unless he wants me to do something. "You're not going to tell me?"

Dec arches an eyebrow as the corner of his mouth tilts up. I don't press further because he'll tell me when he's good and ready.

"Well, did you?"

I shake my head. "Why?"

"Ronnie served him divorce papers today."

I nearly drop the bottle. "Are you serious?"

Dec shoots me an amused smile. "Guess she was so unhappy when Nico told Dad to fuck off, she went and got herself knocked up by Senator Whelan."

Fucking hell. Senator Whelan, Hollywood producer turned politician. "He's got to be at least sixty."

"Fifty-eight. It's all over the tabloids."

I pull out my phone and type in Ronnie's name. Sure enough, this shit is everywhere. "I always knew she was a social climber," I say with a shake of my head. "Good riddance." Dec looks at me oddly. As if he knows something. And for a split second, my heart races. But there's no way he knows what I know about Ronnie, so I let it pass. "How'd you find out?"

"I have Google Alerts set up on all our names."

"So you haven't talked to him yet?"

Dec shakes his head and takes a long draw of his cigar, puffing out his cheeks, then slowly exhaling. "He's probably holed up someplace licking his wounds."

"Does Jason know?"

"I doubt it."

"Who's gonna be the one to break it to him?"

Dec gives me an evil grin. "I'll leave that to you, big brother."

We're triplets. Dec and I are identical. Nico was born first, then me, then Dec. In spite of sharing a womb for nine months and a bedroom for nine years, we're surprisingly distant. But I guess that's what happens when you're born into a family where lies and secrets are the M. O. Trust no-one. Tell no-one. Every man and child, for himself. I don't look forward to breaking the news to Jason. Maybe if I stall long enough, he'll hear it from Dad. Or maybe Nico. Although the irony will be too much for Nico to bear. That much I do know. Nico won't be calling Jason anytime soon. "So tell me about your big deal."

Dec grins. "I bought a building. Several, actually."

"Bully for you."

"On Main."

"Wait, *here?*" I lean forward, incredulous. "Why the hell for?"

"Why the hell not?"

"Isn't that taking diversification a little far?"

Dec shrugs. "Let's just say I was helping a friend."

I'm instantly alert. I smell tail. "Who is she?"

Dec's face remains neutral "I could ask you the same."

Fuck me. It shouldn't surprise me, because we share the exact same DNA. Of course he's found a little action. And of course, he'd know I wasn't going without, either. But I'm not giving up my secret for love or money, or even torture. And Dec won't either. "Tell me about the buildings."

"Nothing much. Decent investments that will appreciate over time. One I'm leasing to a brewer. Big dude, named Mike."

A brewery? Now there's something I could get behind.

"Does he have numbers? I might be interested in going in as a silent partner."

"I'll let him know."

Silence falls between us. I lean my head back onto the chair and shut my eyes, the exhaustion from the day catching up with me. I need a shower and a nap before I sneak back over to Macey's.

Dec's voice startles me awake. "You're snoring."

"Shit. I'm sorry. I'll head in." I rise, but Dec motions me to sit back down.

"Let me guess. The cute little girl with the hot mama isn't as cute as she seems?"

"She's a demon." I grit out. "And she scares the shit out of me. I'm never fucking having kids."

Dec raises his glass. "I'll drink to that." His eyes narrow slightly. "Better not say that too loud around Macey."

He knows.

"It's not like I'm going to do it again," I say vehemently.

Dec's eyes narrow further. "It's her, isn't it? You're tapping her mom."

"You're fucking the blonde from the wedding."

Dec goes still, and I know I'm right. It's like that scene in Pulp Fiction where everyone is pointing a gun at someone's head. "I'm going to need a renter for the house downtown." That's his offer. His bribe for me keeping silent. "Interested?"

"You want me to rent from you?"

He shakes his head. "Nah. Just stay in it so it doesn't get vandalized."

"What do you want in return?"

"Nothing."

I don't believe it for a second. There's definitely going

to be a catch. We're Cases after all. There's *always* a catch. "Nothing?"

Dec drains his glass and sets it down on the arm of the chair before rising. "Just my good deed for the year. Think about it," he calls over his shoulder as he disappears around the corner.

Chapter Twenty-Six

I think about it all evening - through dinner, through my shower, while I shave. And by the time I fire up the truck, my mind's pretty much made up. But just to be sure, I think about it some more, covering all the possible angles. By the time I park across the street from the park, I'm certain.

I walk the four blocks from the park, and Macey meets me at the kitchen door. Maybe it's the harsh light, or maybe I'm just tuned in differently after my own exhausting day, but Macey looks... tired. Her smile doesn't stretch as far, and I see stress lines around her eyes. "Are you okay?"

She motions me in, speaking in hushed tones. "Long day. And Soph had a hard time going to bed. It seems you impressed her."

My eyebrows shoot up. "You're kidding."

She drops into a chair next to a half finished glass of something red. "Nope. She wouldn't go to sleep because she wanted me to promise you'd come tomorrow." She waves me to join her.

I gulp, feeling sweat break out on the back of my neck. There's no way I can survive another day like today. I'm wrecked. Not to mention scared shitless that the kid is going to get herself killed on my watch.

"It's okay," Macey reassures me with an amused smile. "One of the other moms agreed to take her tomorrow." It's only then I see an empty glass next to the wine bottle. "Wine?" she asks, motioning to the glass.

I shake my head. "I don't drink wine to unwind."

"I understand."

I don't think she does. And she won't, because that's a can of worms I refuse to open. "How about a tumbler of the Midleton Bluebell?"

She starts to push away from the table, but I lay a hand on her forearm. "You sit. I'll get it."

"Third cupboard from the left."

I find the bottle next to four Waterford crystal glasses. I snag two and the bottle. "Impressive." I motion to the glasses as I prepare to pour.

"Thanks. They were a wedding gift."

My hand stills, but only for a split second. Still, she notices and gasps. "I'm sorry. I didn't mean-"

"It's okay," I say with a wave of my hand. I jealously wonder if she thinks of her late husband when she's drinking the booze I gave her. It's petty and small, but I can't help it. And it reinforces why emotional attachments are a no-go. Too messy. Too complicated. I bring the booze to the table and set a glass in front of her. "I presumed you'd enjoy a little?" Her eyes look sad, and that stupid ache blooms in my chest. I want nothing more than to pull her into my arms and kiss away her expression.

She raises her glass. "Cheers." We both take a sip. It's smoother than my bourbon of choice, but no less complex, and I ponder the nuances as we sip. The silence settles around us like a blanket. After a while, she lets out a heavy sigh and shakes her head. "I'm sorry. I don't mean to be so low energy tonight."

"Should I go?" I don't want to.

"You can't spend the night, but I'd like it if you stayed a while."

I rise and come behind her, dropping my hands to her neck. I move her copper locks to the side, exposing her neck, and start to work at the knots. I've never noticed them before, but tonight, they stand out like a neon sign. How could I have missed them?

She drops her head with a groan and rolls her shoulders. "That feels heavenly." Her voice catches.

It dawns on me that it's probably been a very long time since she's received touch like this. The nurturing "I see you" kind of touch that acknowledges hard work and exhaustion - both physical and emotional. I pause my ministrations as the weight of that sinks in. My stomach flutters way up in my sternum, but I bat the sensation away. This isn't emotion, it's foreplay. Plain and simple. And I pride myself on being an attentive lover. I continue working the muscles, letting my fingers slip below her neckline. "Come on," I say gruffly when the tension has drained from her shoulders. I pull back the chair and bend, sweeping her up into my arms.

"End of the hall on the right," she murmurs as I carry her through the kitchen. She buries her head into my shoulder with a sigh. The door creaks open and I enter her bedroom, as prim and tidy as she is - white sheets, a rocking chair next to the queen-sized bed, and a simple dresser with a mirror perched on top. I step into the space, then quietly push the door shut with my foot. It catches with a quiet *click* and we're home free.

I gently place her on the bed, as if she's antique porcelain. She reclines onto her elbows, and the soft cotton tee-shirt that clings so sweetly to her curves rides up to expose the gentle curve of her belly. There's a vulnerability about her tonight that tugs at me. But I don't want to analyze it. I just want to make her feel good. To erase some of the day's hardship with pleasure and release.

Our lovemaking is soft and slow. I take my time with her body, serenading her with my mouth, my tongue, until her little gasps and ragged breaths, and quiet moans tell me she's nearly there. When I hover over her, she looks up at me with luminous eyes. My breath sticks in my throat. I can't breathe as I stare down at her.

"Thank you," she murmurs, as she pulls me in for a deep, searing kiss. I slide into her slowly, losing myself in the sensation, pushing away the urge to run. Instead, falling deeper and deeper into her as our bodies move together, our release sweeping us away like a riptide.

"I'VE TARGETED A VINEYARD," I say a few days later when I walk into Jason's office. He grunts but doesn't look up from his laptop. I toss the folder down on his keyboard. He looks up with a scowl but takes it, flipping through it, and pausing every couple of pages.

"Why this vineyard?"

"They're growing for bulk pinot production only. I think I can do something with it."

"What do you have in mind?"

"Rosé."

Jason's eyebrows rocket. "With pinot?"

"Sure, why not?"

"Because that's a valuable grape to be wasting on rosé."

"Who says it's wasting if it sells?"

He doesn't respond. Instead, he skims more pages. When he's finished the last page, he lays the folder on the desk. He's doing all this deliberately to gain the upper hand, to remind me he's in charge. But it's not going to work this time, because I've done the due diligence. Hell, I even ran my idea by Macey. "What's your plan?" he finally asks.

"We fly out this week for a few days. Check the grapes, let the grower know what we're planning and fly back close to harvest time."

He narrows his eyes. "And when do you expect that?"

"It's been hot and dry this summer. All signs are indicating an early harvest - I'd head out the end of the month and start checking brix levels daily beginning the first week in August."

Jason's jaw tightens. "Depending on how things go, that could coincide with the harvest here. Then what?"

Fuck. I hate it when he runs contingencies. It's not just a military thing either. He used to do this when we were younger, too. Only then, his intent was to box me in. Make me feel small. I won't give into that this time. Not anymore. "Then I'll go it alone."

"Do you honestly think you can do that and make a good wine right out of the gate, with no experience whatsoever?"

"I have plenty of fucking experience," I retort, my own jaw clenching. "It's not rocket science." And I already have a brilliant idea to move the wine once it's released, but I'll be damned if I let Jason in on those plans. I'll be long gone from here by the time the bottles are ready for sale.

Something close to admiration flashes through my brother's eyes. It's a first, and so startling, I almost don't believe it. But then he drops the bomb. "Well good luck, then. I won't be able to go with you this week."

"What? What do you mean? You agreed."

His face is stony, implacable, and right now, I fucking hate him. I should have expected this. "Millie's been put on bed rest. I need to stay here."

"But can't her dad take care of her for a few days?"

Jason glares. "She's. My. *Wife.*"

"We all know what promises mean to you." I spit.

Quick as lightning, Jason's out of his chair and he's pinned me against the wall. "Want to elaborate on that? Asshole?" he snarls.

"You know plenty well what I mean. Asshole." I snarl back. "Wanna punch me out for speaking the truth? Go right ahead. It won't be the first time."

His eyes are as angry and hard as I've ever seen them, and I brace myself for the punch I'm convinced is going to land somewhere above my navel. I silently dare him to take a hit, and he might have done it, too, if not for his phone vibrating next to his laptop. He steps back, flexing his right hand, and checks the text that came in. "Take Macey. Her family owns a vineyard in Upstate New York. She'll be able to help you."

"Is this some kind of a guilt gesture?" I snap. "Because no thanks." I'm playing him a bit here, but I don't want to come across as too enthusiastic. A few days alone with Macey is a fucking windfall, and I'm not going to do anything to make Jason any more suspicious about us than he already is. And although wild horses couldn't drag the admission from me, I'd appreciate her input.

Jason gives me a look of pure disgust. "You know what your problem has always been? You're too cocky for your own good. And one of these days, real soon, it's going to catch up to you." He pokes a finger into my sternum. "And when it does, you better pray to your Higher Power that someone gives a shit." He turns on his heel and exits the office, slamming the door behind him.

Chapter Twenty-Seven

*J*ason is at Macey's when I pull up in the Pagani. It doesn't surprise me, but it *does* irritate the shit out of me. As far as he's concerned this is strictly a business trip, although I have other plans for Macey as soon as we're out of Kansas airspace.

Jason gives me a hard stare as I saunter up the walk, aviators firmly in place. "A little overdressed, aren't you?"

I lift a shoulder. "Maybe, maybe not."

"Do you honestly expect to walk through a vineyard in a linen suit?"

Absolutely, now that he's suggested I shouldn't. "I think I can afford the dry cleaning."

Jason looks like he's about to say something, but slams his jaw shut when hell-child bursts through the front door. I have to admit, she's as cute as a button, and I have no idea why she likes me. She's like a cat who knows you're allergic. And somehow, she's wormed her way into my affection, even if she's trouble with a capital T. "Hi, Austin," she says. "Mommy says you're going to the ocean."

"Not exactly, kiddo. But we won't be far."

"Will you bring me some seashells? I love seashells."

Fact. She has three egg-cartons full of seashells that she's forced me to sort over and over, and over. I've learned enough about seashells, I could be a fucking marine biologist.

"I told you, sweetheart, mommy isn't going to have time to go to the ocean this trip," Macey reprimands as she pulls a small suitcase onto the porch. She's wearing the pink sundress again, the one she wore when she came onto me in the vineyard, and I can't help but wonder what treasure she's hiding under it this morning. She gives me a bland smile before looking to Jason. "My parents will be here this afternoon, is Millie okay?"

I have to admire her composure. Nothing about her body language or her expression conveys we have dirty hot sex on a regular basis. Fleetingly, I wonder what it would be like if people knew about us. If we were a real couple. But that brings unnecessary complications and certain death at the hands of my brother, so I push the thought away as quickly as it enters.

Jason nods. "Emma and Jamey are looking in on her until I can get back." He ruffles Sophie's hair. "And we're gonna go ride bikes over at the park, and after that maybe a horse ride at Uncle Sterling's. How does that sound?"

Sophie bounces and claps. "Will you let me ride no hands like Austin does?"

Two pairs of eyes swivel my direction, one wide and shocked, the other narrow and hard. I raise my hands. "What? She had her helmet on." I can't believe the little hellcat outed me. That was supposed to be our secret. "She was fine. I was right next to her the whole time," I finish defensively. "Gotta let kids push their boundaries. Right Jase?" I give him a meaningful look. "Kind of like jumping off bridges, huh?" I add, referring to the time Jason forced me to jump off the Pope Street bridge in St. Helena when I was eleven.

Macey covers Sophie's ears, seemingly oblivious to the sudden ice that's arisen between me and my dear older brother. "Don't give her any ideas. She's already tried to jump off the shed with an umbrella trying to be Mary Poppins."

Jason shifts his eyes away with a cough. "Don't worry, I'd never let anything happen to Soph. You know that."

Guilty bastard. I have half a mind to call him out and get all the shit out into the open, once and for all.

Macey levels a glare at both of us. "Well, I don't need either of you encouraging her wild behavior."

I grab her suitcase. "She'll be fine, won't you, Sophie?" I offer her a fist bump as I pass, and wink at my brother. "Don't let her do anything I wouldn't do."

Jason utters a throaty growl in response, which draws a chuckle from me. I hold open the passenger for Macey, and give Jason and Sophie a final wave before I slip into my car. Dropping into the low seat is a welcome change from the truck. Like a homecoming of sorts. I've missed the way the leather seat wraps around me like an embrace.

"Did you have to goad him like that?" Macey admonishes as we speed away.

"You don't know the half of it."

"So tell me."

Her challenge lingers in the air as I drive north toward the airport in Manhattan where our private jet waits on the tarmac. But I know better than to open that can of worms with Macey. She loves my brother. Not romantically, but with a fierce kind of familial love that if I examine too closely, makes me jealous as fuck, because he doesn't deserve it. Before I can stop myself, I wonder what it must be like to be on the receiving end of love that strong. A savage longing flashes through me, burning its way across my chest as rapidly as a lightning bolt flashes across the sky, practically gone before it registers. But the taste of it lingers in my mouth.

I place my hand on her knee, sliding it up her leg with a dirty grin, because I'm not dwelling on childhood shit when I have a weekend of pure unadulterated pleasure ahead of me. "I'd hate to ruin your impression of him. And besides, there are other things I'd rather discuss."

"Like what?" She laces her fingers with mine.

"Like what's under that sexy skirt of yours."

Her husky laugh fills the car. "It'll cost you to find out."

"Name your price, Gorgeous."

"Hmmm." She taps her lip in mock speculation. My mind runs in a thousand directions, each of them a sexy scenario involving naked body parts, so when her answer comes in a breathless rush, I'm momentarily stunned. "I want a day in bed - naked, and watching our favorite movies, drinking wine and eating Chinese take-out."

Chapter Twenty-Eight

I blink, taking a moment to process her request. It's... intimate. Frighteningly so. I was prepared to finger her pussy while I drive, not engage in an activity normally reserved for couples in love. The back of my throat tickles as I search for a response. I can feel her eyes on me, expectant and hopeful. The back of my neck heats uncomfortably as the silence becomes heavy. But I can handle this, can't I? It's just fucking with food breaks, and a movie soundtrack in the background. It doesn't have to be... emotional. "Deal." My voice comes out strangled. Tight. *Afraid.* Fuck me, can she hear it? I clear my throat, forcing the conversation back to safer territory. "Now, show me that pretty little pussy of yours, Gorgeous. I wanna see you finger yourself until you come."

Her hands ruck up her skirt, but she stops, mid-thigh. "I-I've never..."

"Masturbated in front of anyone? Good," I growl. At least there's something she'll only have with me. "Are you wet just thinking about it?"

"Yes," she breathes, slowly hitching her skirt higher, hand slipping beneath the pink layers.

"Are you wearing anything under that?"

"No." Her voice catches on a laugh.

"Such a dirty girl," I say roughly. "Show me. Did you shave again? Is your pretty pussy soft and smooth for me?"

Her laughter is sweet and soft, and it turns my cock to steel. She flips up her skirt, and opens her knees.

"Fuck, your cunt is gorgeous."

She draws a finger through the smooth lips and I groan, gripping the steering wheel so hard my knuckles turn white. "Again. Do that again." I swerve, narrowly avoiding a truck that's too close to the center line.

"Eyes on the road, bad boy," she says sharply.

"Tell me what you're doing then. In detail."

That elicits a laugh so full of promise my cock jerks, wanting in on the action. She leans over the console and runs her hand over my length. "I'd hate to distract you from driving." She makes quick work of my belt, button and zipper, and slips her hand inside my shorts, squeezing me and palming my slick, engorged head. My mouth turns to ash. I was supposed to be in charge here. "You're supposed to be touching yourself."

"This is so much more fun," she rumbles.

"Time for me later, Gorgeous. Now stick your fingers inside your hot little cunt."

She releases me with a laugh and I nearly weep from the ache in my balls. She unclips her seatbelt, then slips a foot out of her shoe and places it on the dashboard. "I'm not buckled, so drive carefully."

My speed has slowed to a crawl. For the first time in probably ever, I'm driving the speed limit, a leisurely forty-five miles-per-hour. "I'll be careful," I say tightly.

I quickly glance over and her fingers are dancing over

her pussy lips, circling her clit. "God, you're gorgeous," I say too loudly. I'm sorely tempted to pull over and watch, but the fact that I can't, that we're driving, not to mention the possibility we might get caught by someone who knows Jason, keeps my eyes on the road. Mostly.

"No peeking."

"Then talk." My words come out terse, clipped. I can't talk and concentrate on the road anymore.

"I'm touching my clit."

"Is it wet?"

"Yes."

My cock jumps. I know she sees it because she sucks in a breath and hums in the back of her throat. "How wet?" My voice is so strained I don't recognize it.

She reaches over and paints my lower lip with her arousal. "Very." I nip at her finger, sucking it into my mouth and lapping her essence like I'm starving. The taste of her, the scent of her, only makes me want more. It's sweet and sharp, a picture of contrasts, and I'm addicted to it. My hand drops to my cock, and I pump once, twice, just to take off the edge. "I thought I was supposed to do that."

"Then get to it baby. A man can only take so much." With another breathy giggle she brings her hand back to her core. I hear the second she slides into her slick, hot channel. "One or two?"

"Two," she answers on a gasp. The sound of her fingers slipping in and out of her hungry pussy is the most erotic thing I've ever heard.

I sneak a look. I can't not look. Not when Macey is fingering herself in my car as we fly down the road. It's as beautiful as I imagined - her first and second fingers coated with her juices, her mouth open, tongue fluttering against her lower lip, eyes half-lidded, as she brings herself closer and closer to the edge. "Fuck that's hot. Where'd you learn to do that?" She smiles like there's some secret part of her that I don't know about.

I want to know about it. I want to know all of it. And not because I'm going to explode into a million pieces if I don't sink my cock into the place it calls home, right now.

Her breath comes faster, and her hips are pumping as she chases down her orgasm. My cock responds, energy spooling and coiling in my balls ready to release the second I relinquish the iron-control I'm exerting not to come like a thirteen-year-old who's never been touched. "I'm… close," she squeezes out, voice rising in a moan. "I'm… coming. Oh *jesusfuckingshit I'm COMING.*" Her face is the picture of perfection, frozen someplace between a beatific smile and a grimace of pain. Her body shudders as the waves take over and her eyes fly open in surprise. No words come from her, only ecstatic sounds as she shudders and bucks.

"Hang on, baby." I hit the brakes and pull over. As soon as the car comes to a stop, I jam it into park with a silent apology I'm treating her so forcefully. I slam the seat backward and reach for Macey. It's not graceful, but the only thing that matters is that we end this together. She climbs on top of me straddling my hips and sinks into me at the same time I thrust up with a grunt. We both gasp at the intensity of it.

Her voice breaks and she stutters. "God… so… full." And then her mouth is on mine, her fingers clawing at my head, her tongue fucking mine as she rides me hard. She's an animal, a wild woman as she takes her pleasure on my cock, rocking and twisting. The scent of our sex fills the car and it's heady, and warm, and I want to lose myself in this moment. I never want it to stop, I never want to stop seeing Macey, I never want to be with anyone else. I shut my eyes against the perilous thoughts, the thoughts that could bring me to my knees, or worse, break me. But they're there, with each thrust and hitch of our hips, snowballing into an avalanche of feelings I can no longer deny and don't have the power to reject. "Austin," she cries out, freezing, then collapsing with a groan as tremor after tremor shakes her body.

Her cunt squeezes me like a vice, pulling everything I have from inside me, wringing me from the inside out. My eyes fly open and our eyes lock. I'm powerless to look away, powerless to stop the emotions flooding through me. Her gaze tells me she feels it too as I let go with a roar, emptying my come into her womb with the ferocity of a lion. I'm shattered, consumed, burned to ash. I'm in love with Macey McCaslin and I'm scared to fucking death.

Chapter Twenty-Nine

We're late to the plane.

I feel off-kilter, unsettled by what transpired in the car. What am I supposed to do now? This is a fling. With a term-limit. I'm not relationship material, and I'm sure as hell not father material. There's no place for this to go. It has to end. But that's the last thing I want.

Macey lays a hand on my arm once I hand off the suitcases to the flight attendant. "Are you okay?"

I've never been so relieved for the protective shield of sunglasses. I toss her a smile as I help her up the stairs to the plane. "Never been better." *Liar.*

Her jaw drops as she turns in a circle inside the plane. "Wow. This is… just, wow."

"It will ruin you for other air travel." I cross to the bar and help myself to a tumbler of Pappy. Ask me if I give a shit that it's ten-thirty in the morning. I lock my elbow to keep my hand from shaking and take a sip, pouring all my focus into the warm, fuzzy feeling as the liquor slides down my throat.

"You're going to be great. You know wine and grape growing better than you think you do."

Her sweetness is like a knife to my heart. She's trying to be supportive, encouraging. She thinks I'm freaking out about the wine. "Come here," I say gruffly, and open my arm. I drain the tumbler with a silent apology to Pappy. Pappy Van Winkle shouldn't be gulped, but this is an emergency. I kiss the top of her head, drinking in the citrusy scent of her that simultaneously lowers my blood pressure and sets my heart hammering. There's no way out of the mess I've created for myself. And if I continue to think about it, I'll need to be committed. So I do what any self-respecting asshole in my situation would do. I fuck Macey's brains out the entire flight to California.

THE VISIT to the vineyard can only be described as hellish. The grapes are overgrown and it's too late in the growing season to thin them now. The damage has been done. I'm outraged that my father, with all of his talk about preserving a 'family legacy' has allowed his vineyards to be so abused. I see the board now for what it's always been - a bunch of sycophants kissing up to the CEO in order to keep themselves in the manner they've become accustomed to. And he accused *me* of sucking off the family teat?

This must show on my face because the head grower pales. "You're fired," I snarl. "Pack your things and go."

"B-b-but, you can't do that," he blusters. "It's nearly harvest." Then he glares. "Mr. Case will have something to say about this."

"I bet he will. Please inform him the *younger* Mr. Case has made an executive decision." I turn on my heel leaving the grower and Macey to scramble after me.

"He's right, you know. It's suicide to fire him this close to harvest," she says, laying a placating hand on my arm. I don't stop walking.

"This is me, not giving any fucks."

"What if he sabotages the grapes?"

"Then I'll throw his ass in jail. And he won't do that because I'll make sure he gets a very nice compensation package."

"But who's going to oversee the harvest?"

"I'll figure it out," I snap. "At the very least, I can pay an assistant grower who's hungry for a chance at a hideous amount of money to supervise it."

"That's ridiculous."

I stop, and she nearly runs into me. "Is it? I think it's a great idea."

"You always think you can throw money at your problems - that money can solve everything." She gives me an accusing glare. "But it doesn't."

"It sure as hell makes it easier, Gorgeous."

"It won't solve the problem that the harvest won't be great."

"I'll cut my losses. Next year will be better."

"But what about making a top-notch rosé?"

I narrow my gaze. "You know grapes, do you think these grapes are salvageable?"

She frowns and shakes her head. "Not for anything more than cougar juice."

I see how it is now. How we've made our fortune. And it makes my skin crawl. We're better than this. *I'm* better than this. With or without a head grower, these grapes will get harvested and dumped into a vat with tons of other mediocre grapes that will get turned into overpriced cheap wine - the kind that ladies fighting old-age tooth and nail get drunk on so they can't see the wrinkles in the mirror.

I turn and march back to the crushing pad. Workers scatter like roaches when a light's turned on. "You," I call out to the one person remaining. "Come here."

He's a young guy, early twenties at most. "What's your name?"

"Isaiah."

"And what's your job?"

He gulps, and lifts his chin. "I'm an intern. From U.C. Davis. Their wine program," he stutters, obviously terrified.

"And what do you think of what's been going on here?"

He assesses me, and I can see in his eyes he's deciding whether or not to speak the truth. "I… ah… I would have done things differently. But I'm just here to observe," he hastens to add.

"What would you have done differently?"

"I'd have thinned the fruit for starters."

"Go on."

Isaiah goes on to present a fairly textbook idea of what he'd do differently in the following growing season. "And," he hesitates.

"And what?" I cross my arms, mostly just to see how he reacts. I'm impressed by the kid. He's eager. And he has a passion for the grapes that literally pours off him. "I'd consider replanting with pinot, or maybe cab franc."

"But that's a five-year investment."

He dips his head. "Yeah. But I think it's smart. Sangiovese is fickle, and I think the soil's too rich here-even on the south facing slopes at the top of the hill."

I'm fucking impressed. "So how would you like to bring in the harvest? I'll make it very worth your while."

"I'd love to, but I'm not allowed to accept money on an internship."

"How 'bout I pay for your last year of school, and give

you an advance for a job?" Beside me, Macey gasps, but I continue. "I'm going to need someone to oversee pruning and replanting this fall. Can you manage that with your class schedule?"

Isaiah's eyes are wide as saucers. "Y-yes, wow... yeah... that would be great. Really?" his voice cracks on the last word.

I nod, mind made up. "You've got talent, and I need people who are unafraid to speak their minds." I slide a glance over to Macey, whose eyes shine with admiration. My chest warms and puffs under her gaze. She's proud of me. It might be the first non-assholish thing I've ever done. I reach into my wallet and pull out my card. "Here's my info. I'll need a report by tomorrow outlining your plan for harvest, your ideas for pruning and replanting, and a cost estimate for all of it, including your tuition and signing bonus. I'll have someone at legal draw up a contract for you."

Isaiah grins broadly and offers his hand. "Thank you, sir. I-I don't know what to say, but I'll make this the best vineyard you have."

"Glad to hear it. Now if you'll excuse us." I touch Macey's elbow and guide us out of the crushing pad.

Once we're out of earshot, she speaks. "That was... incredibly generous of you."

"That's how money solves problems, Gorgeous."

She stops, and eyes me sternly. "I just realized something about you. It's all an act, isn't it? You like to put on this act that you're in it for yourself, and that you don't care, but you do."

She's alarmingly close to the truth, and I wonder how in the hell she's figured it out when I've gone out of my way to be an asshole. She lays a hand on my shoulder and goes on tiptoe, brushing her mouth along my jawline.

"Don't worry," she murmurs. "Your secret's safe with me."

My chest flutters and I freeze. I have secrets. So many secrets. Secrets that if she knew about, she wouldn't be giving me sweet kisses along my jaw. Secrets that if what we have continues, will undoubtedly come to light, and I don't know who that will hurt more - her or me. I give her a quick peck, then force my feet into action. I can't think about it. I can't think about anything. If I do, I might do something stupid like tell her I love her, and ruin everything. "We need to get back to the car. I've got a spreadsheet with other potential vineyards to target. Movie time will have to wait."

The situation is the same at every vineyard we visit. My agitation grows with each stop. This was supposed to be an in-and-out visit with an extra day built in for sexcapades. We were *not* supposed to be crisscrossing Napa and Sonoma inspecting every vineyard on my spreadsheet.

After the fifth stop of the day, the realization dawns that this was all a sham. I've been set up to fail. All three of us have been set up to fail. Not one of these vineyards could produce an award-winning wine. Not this year, maybe not ever. This was just another of Dad's manipulative little games. He knew all along that none of us would be seeing a penny from our funds. And goddammit, I'm going to beat him at his own game. We're parked at an overlook way up by Atlas Peak, but I'm too pissed off to enjoy the beauty of the valley below. I shoot off a text to Declan, letting him know what I've discovered. Nico's disappeared off-grid, so I don't bother him. I pick up a rock and hurl it at the trunk of a tree. Then another, and another.

"Stop," Macey barks, hopping out of the car and slamming the door. "Just. Stop."

I spin and glare. "You don't understand."

"I understand enough. I know all about how your father operates. Don't play his games. Jason didn't."

"I'm not Jason," I grit. "And I don't want to be like him. Ever."

"Why not?" she demands, eyes flashing. "Jason is one of the most honorable people I know."

I cover a sarcastic laugh. She doesn't know him the way I do. "Money is power, and I'm not leaving without my inheritance."

"That's always what it comes down to with you, isn't it? Money?"

"Money is power. And freedom. And I'll be damned if I let someone besides me call the shots in my life."

A flash of grief contorts Macey's face, then her eyes go soft. "I understand. Say no more." She lets out a ragged breath. "I have an idea."

A million questions about her response flood my head, but they're not mine to ask. So I push them away, and instead open my hands. "I'm all ears."

"My parents have a friend out here. An old French guy they met in the eighties. He grows about twenty acres of pinot noir, and typically sells to negociants. He's old school, and you'd have to negotiate with him, make him an offer he can't refuse. And you need to know you'll piss off a few other wineries if he goes with you."

"Are the grapes good?"

"He sells to some of the most exclusive vineyards in the area."

"Let's go."

Chapter Thirty

*M*acey directs me up a winding old dirt road on Mount Veeder. A wizened old farmer meets us at a steel gate.

"Bonjour Marcel," Macey calls as she jumps out of the vehicle. Marcel's face breaks into a wide smile and he opens his arms wide.

"Bonjour ma petite choux. Comme ça va?"

"Bien, ça va bien, merci." She kisses him on both cheeks, and takes him by the hand, bringing him around to my side of the car.

"Marcel, I would like to present to you my friend Austin Case."

Lover I think darkly.

Marcel's eyebrows disappear into his hairline, and he rattles off something in French to Macey that I don't understand - a combination of surprise and agitation.

"Yes, yes, I know. Austin's different. He appreciates the art of winemaking."

I do? Macey gives me a sideways look that says I better. And I guess, in a meta sense, I do. I appreciate the craftsmanship that goes into an excellent IPA, or a Pappy Van Winkle. So yeah, sure. I care about winemaking, too. But only so far as it gets me what I want.

Marcel motions up the hill. *"Vien, vien.* You can park just inside the gate."

He shuts the gate behind me and I step out to join them. The first thing that hits me is the hint of salt in the air. Not as salty as it is in parts of Sonoma, but the hint of ocean air is present at the top of Napa's highest mountain. The air is different here, softer than at our family's estate in Napa proper. Fresher. Cleaner. The kind of air that allows a man to think. I follow the pair up a hill, past a cottage that has seen better days, and a large barn that has been meticulously maintained. I catch up to Macey and Marcel, chattering happily away in French at the edge of a rolling vineyard that appears perched on the top of the world.

Macey shoots me an excited smile. "Nice, isn't it?"

"Come, come." Marcel leads me down a row and stops. "Merlot. Ready late September, maybe October?"

"What other grapes do you have?"

He gives a very Gallic shrug. "Chardonnay, Cabernet Sauvignon, Cabernet Franc."

"Anything ready to harvest in August?"

"Ici? Sur la montagne?" He shakes his head. *"Non, non.* The grapes. They are like a beautiful woman. They need time to be ready."

I had planned to be free of all this by then. But beggars can't be choosers, and I can tell the vines have been meticulously maintained. "Name your price." I blink at the number, but remain silent. He who speaks first loses the negotiation.

Marcel's mouth turns up slightly. He knows the game. He turns and surveys the view. Macey looks back and forth between us, brow furrowed. I turn, too. The view is spectacular. Hills dropping into hills, some cleared for vines, others wild. Redwoods tower in places, and in the distance I hear an eagle cry. It's the kind of view that demands an audience, that asks to be shared. And as I study the stooping muscles of Marcel's aging shoulders, I'm struck by how lonely, how isolated he must feel, up here tending his vines.

I don't know why, maybe it's because I've been off my game since Macey rode me like a woman possessed this morning, but I speak first and offer half.

Marcel's head drops back with a hearty laugh that rings over the fields. He looks at me, then starts again, until all three of us are laughing. When calm returns, he shakes his head. *"Non,"* he says firmly. *"Non."*

I offer higher and he eyes me like I'm a crazy man. "I lost well over a million dollars last year due to the fires. This year you lucky to get any grapes."

I look out at the view again, contemplating. The guy probably has as much in the bank as I do. But he's right, his grapes will be in high demand this year. He could ask twice what he asked and probably get it. And in the end, it's a small price to pay for my freedom. Lose the battle, win the war. I offer my hand and quote his opening offer. Macey bounces on her toes, just like her mini-me, and I'm glad she's here, that she's shown me a new slice of heaven so close to my own backyard.

———

"PASS THE GENERAL," I ask, referring to the General Tso takeout that Macey's been scarfing as the credits to *Reservoir Dogs* begin to roll. It's two p.m. and we haven't left the bed since we collapsed into it the night before, a tangle of limbs after the chef's tasting meal at The French Laundry. But that's what happens when dinner becomes a three-hour exercise in foreplay.

"There's not much left," she says with a sheepish grin as she passes the nearly empty container.

"I'm gonna have to spank you for that," I say, as I cue up *Pulp Fiction*. Watching Tarantino with her has been yet another surprise in the long line of surprises that is Macey. She laughed, my god did she laugh - rich, full belly laughs - in between devouring the enormous order of takeout we had delivered to the room.

Her eyes twinkle wickedly. "Oh, please, no," she covers her mouth coquettishly in mock fear. "I promise I'll make it up to you."

"Good," I say between bites. "I have some ideas."

"So do I." Her hand slips beneath the sheets and skates along my thigh.

I finish the General with a smack of my lips, and place the empty container on the bedside table. Even after hours of relentless lovemaking, I'm still not sated. I don't think I'll ever be sated. Yet, with each kiss this morning, each touch, each heated glance, I know we're marching closer and closer to our end. I fucking hate it.

She rolls over on her side running the flat of her palm across my belly. Across my chest, exploring with a touch that's both curious and sensual. And then her fingers find them - the dual scars to the side of my left pec, just under my armpit. Most of the time, I forget they're there. But her sensitive fingers find the discrepancy in the flesh and her eyes widen. "What's this? What happened?"

My belly tightens. I haven't thought about the incident in ages, but the remembered pain lights my nerve endings like it was yesterday. I shut my eyes, but all I see are the dust motes floating in the air, highlighted by the cracks in our barn.

"Austin? Are you okay?"

I hear the fear in her voice, the concern, but even that isn't enough to draw the story from me. "It's nothing." I shrug it away, pulling her hand to my sternum, clasping it, holding it against my pounding heart. "Happened a long time ago."

"Who was it? Who hurt you?"

"Doesn't matter."

But she won't let it go. "Whoever it was, they deserve the ninth circle of hell for burning you like that. How old were you?"

Eleven. But I deflect by rolling us over and pinning her to the bed, and covering her with kisses. She's smart, my gal. But then again, it's easy to recognize a cigarette burn. Not much else is that small and that perfectly round.

"They don't deserve protecting, Austin," she says, unwilling to let it go.

I pause and look down, ready to drown in the feeling I see emanating from her beautiful green eyes. I wonder if she'd say that if she knew who gifted me with the twin scars. But I refuse to be pulled down into the murky quicksand of my childhood. Her hand comes to my cheek and the action is so compassionate, so filled with love, that I stop breathing. I can literally feel my chest tightening as the air in my lungs goes stale.

"You deserved better," she whispers, eyes searching mine.

I feel like I've been drawn and quartered, like my heart is going to spill out on the bed along with my guts, a steaming pile of goo. A part of my brain is frantically calling time-out. Begging me to stop, but I can't. I won't. I've crossed some mysterious line in the sand I didn't even know existed, and I can't go back.

I can't go forward either, and the pain of that is almost

too much. So I choose now. I drop my head, mouth brushing against hers, tongue teasing for entrance. I take solace in our coupling, find absolution in her touch. If now is all I get, then I will take everything from this moment and then some. I will ruin Macey for anyone else, the same way she's ruined me.

Chapter Thirty-One

*W*e return to Prairie subdued. Sure, some of that has to do with the fact that we fucked like rabbits for three days, full stop. But something has shifted between us. The glances exchanged when no one's looking are longer, more meaningful, and tinged with goodbyes. I double down on my efforts to make every tryst memorable, better than the last.

We're screaming into crush season, and thanks to Millie's enforced bed rest, Jason has placed us in charge of calling the harvest for the cab franc. Our vineyard rendezvous have come to an end. We'd surely be caught now, with the buzz of activity. Millie's father, Mike, has already called harvest for his Chardonel grapes, and since this is a small operation, no one is exempt from picking. There's an energy in the air that's contagious. Macey is in full-blown winemaker mode, and it's a sight to behold. No wonder Jason brought her on board, she's so much more than a somm. She's everywhere at once, first consulting with Mike, then literally running into the vineyard to check brix levels.

I catch her on her way back from the vineyard. "Shall I go pick up Sophie?"

She gasps and checks her phone, then smacks her forehead. "OhmygodIcan'tbelieveIforgottopickupSophie." She pauses for a breath, looking mortified. "Are you sure?"

"Of course."

"But you don't have a car seat."

"Give me your keys."

"They're in the ignition." She leans up on tiptoe as if she's going to kiss me, then catches herself, and looks over her shoulder with a small laugh. She turns back around and grimaces. "Wow, that was close."

Yeah, wow. I'm almost at the point that I don't care if Jason finds out. Almost. I nod and clear my throat, jamming my hands in my pockets and rocking back on my heels. "Yeah. We can't get careless." She wants to kiss me. I can feel it. Hell, *I* want to kiss her. I can already feel her breath tickling the corner of my mouth, the brush of her plush lips.

She presses her lips together and nods, eyes downcast. "Yeah." She sucks in a breath and lets it out on a sigh. "Okay. Well, I've gotta run." She takes a step back and meets my eyes with a tiny, sad smile. "Thank you."

I ruminate on her expression the entire drive into town. There's an elephant in the room that neither of us wants to acknowledge.

"Where's mommy?" Sophie asks suspiciously when I arrive at the day camp.

"She's working."

"But she *always* picks me up," she says with a quivering lip.

Oh jesusitschrist. If she starts crying, I'm fucked. I'm not equipped for wiping away women's tears, no matter what their age. Spoiling, yes. Lovemaking, undoubtedly.

But tears? Fuck no. But I also know that Sophie is tough as nails, and something must have happened today at camp if she's close to tears. I squat down so she's at eye-level. "I know, kiddo. So how about chocolate shakes at the diner?" That seems like the perfect way to spoil a precocious five-year-old.

She immediately brightens. "But mommy doesn't let me have ice-cream unless it's a special occasion."

"Don't you think me picking you up from camp is a special occasion?"

Her devilish smile is back in place. She likes my logic. Was Macey like this as a little girl? All vim and vigor, running wild through her parents' vineyard, climbing trees and causing trouble for the adults in charge of her safety? Could she have been bought off with a chocolate shake? I'll never know, because we've never talked about her childhood. But at least I can spoil Sophie this once.

I rise and she slips her hand into mine. I brace against the tug I feel deep in my chest, the feelings of protectiveness that arise as I give her tiny hand a squeeze. "C'mon. Let's go."

She skips to the car and climbs into the backseat. "Wait," she says as I move to shut the door. "You're supposed to check it's buckled."

"Looks like it to me," I say, eyeing her.

She scowls. "You're *supposed* to."

I bend across her and give the seatbelt a tug. "Satisfied?"

She nods with a self-satisfied grin. We drive about a block before she speaks up again. "You're supposed to ask what I did today."

I catch her eye in the rearview, and she's waiting expectantly for the question. "What did you do today?"

"I threw sand at Aiden and got sent to time-out," she says proudly.

My eyebrows launch to my hairline. *"You threw sand at Aiden?"* My immediate response is relief that I'm the one to learn this. I'm pretty sure Macey would shit bricks if she found out Sophie was picking fights, and I wonder why nobody from camp called her. Of course, if they had, she'd have ignored the call anyway, or missed it. Cell service isn't so hot in the middle of the vineyards. "And *why* did you throw sand at Aiden?" I ask sternly. I should be stern about this, right? Throwing sand is bad. Very bad.

She shoots me a defiant, half-fearful look, and her lower lip starts to quiver again. "Because he said I don't have a daddy."

Little fucker. I don't care who Aiden is, or whether or not he's mostly a nice kid, I want to pound his puny little head into the ground for making Sophie cry. I clear my throat. "But you do have a daddy, right, kiddo?"

She nods solemnly. "He's in heaven, but Aiden said that didn't count."

"Fuck Aiden."

Sophie's eyes widen. "You're not supposed to say bad words."

"And you're not supposed to throw sand, but you did it anyway." God, I hope Macey doesn't hear about this. She'll be beside herself. And then she'll be pissed at me for teaching her daughter four-letter words.

Sophie studies me through big round eyes. "I miss my daddy."

Kill me now. I feel for her, but I'm the wrong guy for this job. I don't know what to say. I clear the frog from my throat. "I bet you do. And you know, no one can take your daddy from you, right? No one." I hope it's enough. I don't like the bastard, and not because of what I remember of him, vague though it may be. He broke Macey's heart. His daughter's, too. But I'll be damned if I crush a little girl's dreams of her father, even if he was an asshole who left them high and dry.

"No one," she repeats softly, looking absolutely crestfallen.

I clench the steering wheel as my heart does loop-de-loos. I know that heartache. That pain of loss and betrayal. "Time for shakes," I say roughly, pulling into the diner parking lot a little too fast.

"French fries too?" She asks hopefully.

"Sure. What the hell. French fries too."

"You said a bad word," she points out.

"Yep. I did. Grown up's prerogative."

She clambers out of the booster seat and this time I offer my hand. She takes it firmly. "What's pero... pero..."

"Prerogative?"

She nods.

"It means it's my choice to say those words." That satisfies her long enough for us to walk into the diner and settle into two stools at the long Formica counter.

Sophie waves. "Hi, Dottie."

Dottie, the town matriarch and command center for all the gossip, bustles over to the counter. "Well hi there, sweetie pie. How are you today? Your mama busy with the vineyard?"

"I threw sand," she confesses, looking not one bit apologetic.

"Did you now? And what does your mama have to say about that?" Dottie gives me a healthy dose of stink-eye, as if it's my fault she threw sand at day camp.

"I haven't told her," she mumbles.

"I see." Dottie pats down her apron and harrumphs. "Well, nothin' that some pie won't cure, I suppose."

Sophie's eyes glow. "Chocolate shakes? With fries?"

"That too, I suppose." She turns to me, still looking suspicious. "And for you?"

"Same."

"Alrighty, you two sit tight." She hurries off, hollering something through the kitchen window.

I'm at a loss for what to say now that it's just the two of us. I pat Sophie on the head and watch quietly as she colors the kiddie menu. Fortunately, Sophie's not in a talking kind of mood, and she's content to connect the dots and color flower petals, drawing her own additions to the picture in the margins.

The shakes and fries arrive, and Sophie's very happy to dip her fries into her shake and make airplanes into her mouth. I might have to revise my first impression of her. She's definitely grown on me. Hell, I'll probably miss her when I go. I think mostly I'll miss her because of the way she reminds me of her mother - the mischievous looks, the naughty grins, the fire in her eyes when she's mad about something. "Come on, kiddo. Time to get you back to your mother," I say when she slurps up the last of her shake from the bottom of the tall glass.

"But you didn't finish yours." She eyes my half-consumed shake intently.

"Oh, no. Don't get any ideas. You're already on a sugar high."

"Please?" she wheedles, eyes going soft.

I have to laugh. But I shake my head. "Car. Your mom's probably worried."

But Macey's nowhere to be found when we arrive back at the vineyard. Not waiting by the drive, or at the crushing pad, or even in the office. I send her a quick text: *Back w/ S where ru?*

Five minutes later, she still hasn't responded.

Sophie's oblivious, already halfway up a tree in the yard. "Yes, I see you," I shout. "Be careful up there."

Ten minutes later, I text again: *ru okay?*

Not thirty seconds later, she hurries into the yard, breathless. "There you are," she says brightly. Too brightly. Immediately, I'm on alert.

"You okay?"

She nods, not meeting my eyes. "Sorry, I was out in the fields, we're going to harvest the cab franc tonight."

"Tonight?"

She nods. "Brix are at twenty-three, and a storm system is projected to move in late morning, tomorrow. We've gotta start tonight."

I hear the excitement in her voice, even as I deflate a little. So much for the back rub I'd planned to give her tonight. It could wait, the grapes couldn't. "Great. What about Sophie?"

"She's got a bedroom across the hall from Jason and Millie. She'll be fine here tonight." She cocks her head, looking at me funny. "You know, you're really great with her."

"Yeah? Why do you say that?"

"She talks about you all the time."

"Only because I curse in front of her."

She laughs. "Seriously, you'd make a great dad someday."

Something in her voice puts me instantly on guard. "Who me?" I shake my head. "No way."

Her brows knit together. "You really think that?"

I laugh harshly. "I know that, Gorgeous."

"So… you're fling material, not father material." Her voice goes flat. Emotionless. She frames her comment as a statement, not a question, and then I swear she mumbles "Good to know now." Something about this whole exchange feels off. But I can't put my finger on it. She flashes me a smile, only it doesn't reach her eyes.

"Something like that," I joke. Only not really. My thoughts turn to the pact Declan and I made, to never have children. To never let the sins of the father, or the brother, be passed on to the son. But I can't exactly explain that to Macey.

Chapter Thirty-Two

*T*he harvest is in. The grapes have been crushed, and the second bottling of Stardust Rosé is complete, no thanks to Jason, who was more or less absent. Mike's chardonel grapes are slowly fermenting in a steel tank at fifty-five degrees.

I've been a visitor at Macey's house so much in the last three weeks that she's stopped insisting I walk over, or park in the alley. I stop on the way back to her place and grab a box of take-out. My ladies are hungry and tired, and the least I can do is supply dinner. Macey shoots me a grateful glance when I walk into the kitchen with a box full of take-out, and a grocery bag full of ice-cream and Oreos in the other. Sophie immediately eyes the ice-cream. "Dinner first," I growl. I'm already impatient to send her off to bed so that I can have Macey to myself. Sophie just giggles and climbs up into her seat, not intimidated by my bear-like demeanor in the least.

Somehow, we manage to get Sophie put to bed with only two bedtime stories. Then I entice Macey into a hot shower and proceed to love her until the knots work themselves out of her neck. After, I wrap her in a towel and carry her back to the bedroom. But she scrambles down before I can shut the door. "Be right back." She scoots down the hall, naked as the day she was born and disappears into the kitchen.

I settle myself between the cool sheets to await her return. If she brings the ice-cream, I'm licking it off her belly. Her feet slap on the wood floor as she pads back holding a bag of Oreos. Her mouth bows as she shuts the door with purpose then slips in next to me and props herself up with pillows, leaving the bag in her lap. She fishes a cookie out of the package and slowly twists it, then pops the unfrosted piece of cookie into her mouth, licking the crumbs from her bottom lip.

"You're not supposed to eat cookies in bed." I lick a crumb she missed from the corner of her mouth.

She gives me a saucy arch of her brow and lifts her delicate shoulder. "It's my bed. I can do what I want."

"But what about crumbs? No crumbs in my bed," I pronounce with the authority of a king. Unless, of course, I was licking them off her body.

She licks the frosting off the remaining cookie. My shaft gives a painful throb, swelling at the sight of her pink tongue moving in slow circles, lapping up the sugar paste. It's erotic as fuck, and I want her to look at me just like that the next time she takes me in her mouth. Like I'm dessert. She gives me a Mona Lisa smile, but I see the want building in her eyes. She drops her gaze to my burgeoning cock, and nibbles at the cleaned off cookie. "You're just a visitor. My bed, my rules."

Something I can't identify balloons inside my chest. Something that arrows down into my belly and makes me squirm. I don't want to be a visitor. I want… more. I want to be setting the rules. Calling the shots. It's my preferred role. Hell, it's my fucking destiny. I take what's left of the cookie and bring it to my mouth, swallowing it whole.

"Hey, that was mine."

Her lower lip juts out and I can't resist taking a nibble of that, either. I can't resist floating a trial balloon. "What if… I wasn't just a visitor… what if…" I trail hot kisses down her neck. "I called the shots for a while, see how it goes?"

She goes still, frozen as a deer in headlights. Fuck. I've completely misjudged the situation. After a sickeningly long pause, she sniffs. "I… umm… I don't think you're ready for that."

Her answer reminds me of the night I met her, when she was trying to be tactful about her distaste for my family's wine. She's trying to be tactful now, but I'm done with being polite. Done with not talking about the elephant in the room, done with the innuendos and the taboo subjects. Finito. Caput. "*Au contraire*, Gorgeous. I think *you're* the one who's not ready. You're the one still hung up in the past."

Her eyes flash. I've poked the bear, and she's going to unleash her fury. "Really?" Her voice drips with disdain. "You're accusing *me* of being stuck in the past."

It's a rhetorical question, but I rise to the bait. "It's the truth, isn't it? You're too afraid to confront your past and move on."

Her eyes darken. "You want the truth?" Her voice is knife sharp. "To coin a phrase, I don't think you can handle the truth."

I lean in, breath coming in shallow pulses. "Bring it, Gorgeous. You think you know everything about me? About what I can and can't handle? Bring it the fuck on."

"Fine." She rucks up the sheet, covering her breasts like she's putting on armor. "Know what happened the last time I let someone else call the shots? When I trusted someone to be there?" She twists the sheet in a knot. "He killed himself. You know what Veteran's benefits are like? They're shit. The policy his parents took out on him? Void in the case of suicide. And there was no way it could be ruled accidental. Not with his brains splattered all over the kitchen wall." Her voice catches, and a flush creeps down the back of her neck. She glances up, eyes glimmering and dark, lost in a memory so painful, she doesn't see really see me. "The man I loved, the man who I gave *everything* to, checked out and left me to clean up the mess. Literally." The story her eyes tell punches me in the gut, and I find it hard to breathe. She doesn't have to fill in the blanks, it's as plain as day between us. She scrubbed the walls clean herself.

My belly gives a sickening lurch, as the lurid visual dances before my eyes. I want to gather her into my lap, pet her like a lamb and promise her everything is going to be all right. That I'd never leave her high and dry. That I'm her knight in shining armor, her champion. But it would be a lie. Sophie starts kindergarten in a week, and once the grapes are barreled I'm on the first plane back to California. The air is heavy and raw between us, filled with unspoken words, of might haves and hopes burned to ash. I want to say something, but any words of comfort would come off as trite. Insincere, even if I meant them. Because she's right. This shit is too heavy for me to handle. I can't promise her the fucking fairy tale with the happy ending. There is no happy ending for us, and the reality of that settles into my bones with cold certainty. Somehow, when neither of us were looking we went from fucking to…

being friends… to something far, far deeper. And now it's complicated, messy. Like cookie crumbs in bed.

So I do what any self-respecting asshole in this situation would do. I confess something I know without a doubt, will make her hate me.

Chapter Thirty-Three

The words stick in my throat, caught in the tight squeeze behind my tongue. Is this what deathbed confessions feel like, when the secret has become to heavy to bear alone? Possibly, but I doubt I'll find relief at the end of my confession. Certainly not absolution.

"It must bring you comfort to wear your grief like a badge," I say cruelly. She flinches, and the knife in my stomach gives a sharp twist. "To cloak yourself in words like honor. Fidelity."

She gives me a sharp look.

"You accuse me of not being able to handle the truth when you refuse to see the ugly truth about Jason staring you in the face."

Her cheeks darken. "You're just jealous," she accuses.

She's not wrong. Jason's part of her inner circle, though I'm the one she turns to for baser desires. And that's the crux of it. "Everyone's always loved Jason," I begin. "Jason the heir, Jason the West Point star, Jason the wounded warrior. Poor Jason, abandoned by his fiancée."

"And your point is?" She glares. She sits taller in the bed, on guard and ready to defend.

"He's not Jesus Fucking Christ. He's as much of an asshole as the rest of us."

"How dare you say that after all he's been through?" she bristles.

"Because it's the truth. You want the unvarnished truth, Gorgeous? Jason was sent to West Point to shape up. He was a fucking liability to the family."

Her mouth hardens to a thin line. "That's not true."

"Deny all you want, sweetheart. Keep your blinders on if you want, but the fact of the matter is that Jason was the biggest, meanest asshole of all of us. Where do you think Nico learned his tricks?" *Where do you think I learned mine?* I think, resolved to spare her from the worst of my brother's transgressions. As if taunting me, the two little scars under my arm throb painfully.

"Nico knocked up Jason's fiancée."

"They were already over. Maybe not officially, but I caught Jason in the barn fucking one of Ronnie's friends the day before his last deployment."

"You're lying," she says in a terrible voice.

"Ask him why he refuses to wear his class ring."

She turns the full force of her fury on me, like a goddess ready to incinerate a mortal with a single look. "You. Are. Lying," she punctuates viciously.

I stick to my guns, determined to see this through to its awful end. "Ask him." I know she will, too, because I see the second she realizes I'm not bluffing. I may be slightly exaggerating the circumstances - the girl was giving Jase a BJ, but fucking was definitely on the menu that afternoon - but it's truth enough and has the desired outcome. It's made her hate me, and now I can leave with a clean conscience. Better this way than leaving with her pity. In time, she'll forgive Jason a transgression like infidelity. She'd never forgive him the ugly truth of his brutalizing three kids who worshipped him once-upon-a-time. My jaw aches from holding it tight.

And as much as I want to be inside the circle of her deepest affection, I have to accept that Jason and Sterling will always claim that spot in her heart, next to the boy she once loved and who shattered hers. Better that she hates me. At least there's a beach someplace I can lick my wounds. Indefinitely.

Macey's face crumples, and for an awful second I'm filled with regret. I'm not in the business of hurting women, and I've cut her where she's most vulnerable. It's quite possible I'll go to Hell for this, but I can't give in to whatever ounce of compassion is left in me, or whatever hope I clung to for my own happy ending. Not now, because I'm not done. I need to slam the last nail in the coffin with enough force it will never reopen.

"I was pissed as hell at my brother. For all his talk about the cadet code of honor, to lie, to *cheat* like that?" I paused, gathering my courage, because this, *this* is my darkest secret, darker even than the beatings and bullying. Those wounds, at least, are shared by the three of us. "I helped Ronnie get together with Nico." I'm not proud of it. I reacted in anger, and I absofuckinglutely did it to hurt my brother. To get back at him in some small measure for the hurt he leveled on me as a little kid when I worshipped the ground he walked on.

"Get. Out." She cants her head away, refusing to look at me, but points at the door.

I freeze. This is what I wanted, right? To be set free? I'm supposed to feel relief, not empty.

"Out," she repeats in that terrible tone that says so

much more than the syllables she utters. "I never want to see you again."

In case I was wondering.

I slip from between the sheets and pick up my clothing. I walk with purpose around the bed and pause in the doorway until she looks up. The expression on her face tears me apart. I put it there, and for the second time in as many minutes I wonder if I've made the right choice. "Just remember this, Gorgeous, when you stack me up against your husband, against Jase. In all that's passed between us? I've never once lied to you."

I spin away before she has the chance to respond. I tiptoe quietly past Sophie's room, and I can't resist taking a peek at the angel sleeping peacefully on Princess Elsa sheets. I push down the balloon that's pressing against my chest, filled with emotions I don't wish to examine. I let myself out the front door, and step onto the porch, buck naked and proud of it. I don't care if Mrs. T across the street is peeking through the curtains. Let the old biddy have a show. I toss my clothes onto the passenger seat and fire up the truck, revving the engine, not caring that it's after midnight. Let the fucking world know I was here. I give no shits. I speed off with a squeal of the tires. But my dramatic exit is hampered by the truck's sluggish response to a flattened gas pedal. It finally catches a head of steam halfway down the block, only adding to my dark feelings. Fuck my trust fund, fuck Jason, fuck *her*. I could have given her everything she'd ever wanted.

As soon as I get to the house, I throw on my clothes and pull the Pagani out of the garage. I need to think, and I can only do that in a quiet car going one-ten. I make it to San Francisco in record time, stopping only to fill the gas tank and piss. I pull into the valet line at the Four Seasons and stumble out. I don't even know what time it is, or how

I managed seventeen hours behind the wheel without passing out. I bypass the bar and go straight to the elevator, shutting my eyes to the memory of Macey. It's no better when the door opens to my suite - she moves through these rooms like a ghost. I strip down and step into the shower. And even though the heat pummeling my body brings welcome relief, it does nothing to erase the memory of her, the way her hands fisted against the tile as she came. Or the way she dropped her head back into the spray with a satisfied smile. She's everywhere.

And gone.

The force of the realization hits me like a rogue wave, dragging me under so that I can barely breathe. I stagger out of the shower, not bothering to grab a towel and drop face down on the bed. Only sleep will relieve me of the pain that relentlessly hammers me, tossing me like a piece of driftwood in a tsunami. My world fades to black.

Chapter Thirty-Four

I don't know how long I've slept, or what day it is. To be honest, I don't really care. Maybe it's been a week, maybe longer - it's all a blur, and who fucking cares how much time has passed? I've lost everything that matters. The angle of the sun tells me it's late afternoon. My mouth tastes like dog-shit laced cardboard. I stumble out to the living room and pour myself a full glass of Pappy. I drain it in four long gulps, bracing against the fire that burns its way to my gut. Then I sit and wait for the alcohol to hit my bloodstream, to dull the pain that consumes me. Thirty minutes later, relief hasn't come. I pour another glass. I slam it down as fast as I can and throw the glass against the wall with a roar so loud my throat feels like it has skid marks. It shatters spectacularly. The booze hits me with the force of a baseball bat to the head, and I nearly don't make it back to the bed. But my body refuses to give in, refuses to release me from my misery, and I manage to faceplant on sheets that somehow, magically, still smell like Macey.

"AUSTIN," a voice rumbles through the fog.

I lift a hand that feels heavy as lead. "Go 'way," I mumble.

"Austin." This time the voice is accompanied by a shake.

The voice is pulling me back to reality, and I fight it. "No."

"AUSTIN you sorry excuse, wake the fuck up *now."*

I'm unceremoniously yanked up by my shirt collar and dumped on the floor. I'm awake, now. And pissed as hell. Who in the fuck has broken into my apartment? "Whattheeverlovingfuck," I slur as I rise, attempting to sweep the cobwebs from my brain. My brain is having none of it.

I recognize my brother just before his fist makes contact with my face in a punch that sends me spinning back to the floor. Pain explodes below my left eye. I don't think he's broken my eye socket, but I'm going to have a shiner worthy of a prizefighter. I struggle to my feet. "What in the hell was that for?" My tongue feels like wool and I'm slightly dizzy.

"That was for Macey, asshole," he snarls, winding up.

I throw up my fists, but I'm in no shape to be blocking punches. Especially from Jason.

"And this is because you knocked her up you worthless fuck."

His punch hits his mark. My nose breaks with a deafening crunch. The second time in my life my nose has been broken, the second time he's busted it. I drop to my knees with a howl. The pain is blinding, and some part of me knows I deserve this, and worse. But another part of me, the part that's sick to shit of being beat on by an abusive asshole, has had enough. I don't bother to stem the bleeding, I'll deal with that later. I charge, tackling his hips and knock him off balance. He lands halfway in the hall with a crash, head nearly coming in contact with the credenza. "And this is because you're the biggest asshole of them all." My fists pound him, but they don't land hard, and he's trained and alert. My punches are no match for his defensive ability.

With a yell, he flips us, and scrambles to his feet. "Fine. You wanna fight? Let's do this."

I'm gasping for air, but I'm not backing down. Not anymore. "Great," I yell, the taste of blood on my tongue. "Let's talk about how West Point didn't take the asshole out of you. No wonder you ended up in intelligence," I spit. "Good 'ole Uncle Sam finally gave you permission to torture." I wipe the blood from my mouth with the back of my hand so I can keep talking. "How many kids did you make piss themselves because they were so scared? How many?" I'm sure they can hear us three floors below. "Did you tie up their brothers or sisters the way you did Nico? And make them watch while you beat their brothers? Or their parents?"

Jason roars and charges, but I'm ready and I'm not playing fair this time. I sweep his prosthetic and the floor trembles when we land. We're a tangle of fists flying, shouts, and insults. I land a good one on his face, acknowledged by his grunt of pain. Good. Let him feel half of what I felt.

"Did Macey figure out that you gave me the cigarette burns? Did she? Or are you still trying to pretend you're honorable?" Each word comes out broken, punctuated by punches and kicks. "Did you tell her you cheated?"

"I didn't have to, asshole. You did."

I'm losing this fight, just like I always do. While I might

be as big as Jason now, he's still a fighting machine, and I'm not. My m.o. is always to walk, to avoid. Always. But this time, I have nothing to lose, and so I bring it. I struggle to my feet and manage to land a few kicks to his ribs before he's up and charging again. We flip back over the couch, landing dangerously close to the fireplace. I fleetingly wonder if this is a death-fight. We're too stubborn to stop. Neither of us will call uncle. I'll die before I ever say uncle again. I offer a silent apology to Macey. But I'm not done. Not yet. I poke the beast. As hard as I can. "I'm glad I fucked Macey," I say between punches, scanning through the swollen slits of my eyes for something to pound him with.

That sets him off, and his punches fly harder, faster. "You don't deserve her."

Truth. I don't deserve shit. "That may-" my words are interrupted by two powerful hands jerking me off Jason. I struggle to focus. There are people in here. Is that... "Miles?" My voice is as cracked as my lip.

"What in the hell are you two doing?" he shouts.

Jason is being restrained by two big men in black. They're enormous. Some stupid twelve-year-old part of my brain is impressed it takes two people to hold him back. I might not have broken his nose, but I split his cheek and he's gonna have a shiner as pretty as my own.

"This stops now, or I call the cops and have you banned from the building."

"But I own this unit." At least I think I do. The punches have rattled my brain, and now I'm not so sure.

"I don't care if you own the fucking Golden Gate Bridge. I will see to it that you're banned and your unit seized."

"I don't think you can do that. I'll ask Dec. Dec would know. Where's my phone?"

Miles is looking at me like I'm delirious, which I guess I am. "If I tell them to let you go, will you play nice?"

I glare across the room at Jason. He glares back.

"Let me rephrase that," Miles says tersely. "Can you behave, or shall I call the police right now? I'm sure the other guests will be happy to let the two of you duke it out from inside a jail cell."

It's tempting. But I have a more pressing question. "How do you know Macey?"

"McCaslin?" Miles' brows disappear into his hair. "Is *that* what this is about?" He shakes his head. "You've got to be kidding me."

I glare at him.

"Okay, you're not." Miles' hands come to his hips, and he lets out a heavy sigh. "Macey was the youngest person ever to earn the designation of Master Sommelier, which she earned at twenty-three. She was raised on a vineyard in the Hudson River Valley."

"I know that. How do you know her?"

"Strictly professionally. Macey has consulted with us for years. Since before her daughter was born."

"Huh."

"Why does this matter?" Jason asks from across the room, still held back by the guards.

"Just curious." I realize the rest of my questions need to be directed at Macey, herself.

"Are you two calmed down enough I can release you?" Miles asks.

I stare hard at Jason. "I'm not done."

"Neither am I."

"But can you finish whatever is going on like civilized men and not animals?" Miles asks, exasperation putting an edge to his usually mild voice.

"Punching isn't my style."

"Could have fooled me," Jason says wryly.

"We'll be fine," I assure Miles, deciding for the both of us.

Miles narrows his eyes. "Do I need to leave a witness?"

Jason eyes me, then slowly shakes his head. "We'll sit across the room from each other."

The guard behind me releases my arms, and I roll my shoulders, working the blood back into my hands. Jason stumbles as he's released, then rights himself.

"I mean it," Miles warns with a hard stare. "Not another sound from up here."

We both nod and stand quietly as the men depart.

Chapter Thirty-Five

*a*s soon as the door clicks shut between Miles and his goons, I pass Jason, hands up and limp to the kitchen. I pull two icepacks from the freezer and grab a couple dish towels from the drawer. "Here." I toss him one as I sit.

"Wait." Jason crosses to me. "Let me fix your nose."

"I can't fucking believe you broke my nose," I mutter.

"It's gonna hurt, but it will heal straight."

"Something else you learned from your torture days?" I snap.

He answers with a growl. "Look up and shut your eyes."

I comply, because I don't want a nose that rivals Quasimodo. He braces his fingers against my cheekbones, then pinches the bridge of my nose. "Count to three."

"One… two…" With a jerk, he snaps my cartilage back into place on two. The pain is so intense my eyes water, but it feels instantly better. "Thanks," I mumble, placing the icepack on my nose. He sits a few feet away and leans back, icepack on his face. I give myself over to the dull pain that envelops my body. We sit in silence until my icepack is no longer cold. I pull myself off the couch with a groan. I'm pretty sure Jason cracked a few ribs. Jason places his icepack into my hand and I hobble to the kitchen and put them back in the freezer. "Beer?" I call.

"Sure."

I crack two local IPAs and return to the couch. We sip in silence.

Jason lets out a heavy sigh. "I'm sorry. I was a shit."

"You were far worse than that." Images flash before my eyes, and with it, the hurt rises. For some reason, I'm reminded of the look on Sophie's face, the day I took her for milkshakes. My heart cracks, and my voice with it. "You have no idea." I shake my head, doing battle with memories and feelings I desperately want to put to rest.

"You're right. I was horrible. And everything you did to me, I deserved. And then some." Jason pauses, and the weight of his confessions sinks in.

"Why?"

Jason gives me a bleak look. "I don't know. I was a kid when my mom died. Younger than Sophie. And you know how Dad is. Emotions aren't part of his vocabulary. And when he married Angelique and she had you three, there was no room for me. I was alone in a way kids should never be alone. I acted out and there was no one to stop me, keep me in line."

He takes a long draw on his beer, gingerly wiping his mouth when he's finished and starts again. "But you're wrong about Johnny and Sterling. They saved me. Millie saved me. I was drowning when I came back to California. Slowly suffocating. I had to get away from Dad, from Angelique, from the memories, the guilt." He drops his head, pressing the bottle to his forehead. "I should have come to you sooner. And I'm ashamed I never did."

The air is heavy between us. I should feel some kind of relief, a sense of closure. After all, this is the apology I've been waiting my whole life for, isn't it? But I just feel empty. And really fucking tired. Then something Jason yelled before my brain kicked into gear registers and hits me with the force of a Mack truck.

"Did you say Macey is… *pregnant?*"

I pull in a deep breath, then another, and another. Pregnant. There's a good chunk of me that's scared shitless at the prospect of being a father. Of the real possibility that I will fail spectacularly at fatherhood. So much so, I think I might pass out. Or be sick. But then I think of Sophie - her spunk, her sparkling eyes, her determination when she's focused on riding her bike or climbing a tree. What if it's another Sophie? Would that be so bad? Not for someone who knows how to be a good parent. But I don't. My role models sucked.

Jason makes a noise of pure disgust. "You could have at least been more careful, for fuck's sake."

"We *were* careful. Fuck, we used double protection at first."

"*At FIRST?*" Jason's look of incredulity is quickly replaced by a scowl. "How long were… wait. Don't tell me," he says with a shake of his head. "I don't want to know."

"Guess I just have super sperm," I say with more than a note of pride. Nothing can stop my little swimmers, apparently. Not condoms, not the pill. I take a perverse kind of pride in that.

Jason stares at me hard, then narrows his eyes. "That was you in the barreling room on my wedding day, wasn't it? I knew it," he says when I don't answer right away.

I poke the bear. I shouldn't, but I can't help myself. I grin. "I don't kiss and tell."

"Fuck you asshole," Jason growls. "That's my best friend's wife."

"Your best friend, who decided it was better to end his life and leave his wife and child broken hearted," I point out caustically.

Jason glares. "Until you've walked in his shoes," he warns.

"It still doesn't change the fact that he abandoned them."

"And you didn't?"

"It was supposed to be a fling."

"And is it, now? Are you going to abandon a child, too?"

"Fuck no," I snap. "I'm not putting a kid through that. No kid should grow up alone. Especially no kid of mine." I'm not exactly sure what that means, though. Macey may be pregnant with my child, but I think there's a pretty good chance she'll tell me to go to hell the next time I see her. My mind spins with the gravity of it. I'll make sure the child is taken care of. Sophie, too. I don't want Sophie to think she's less important. But I'm the worst kind of father material. "I don't know the first thing about being a dad."

"Welcome to the club," Jason retorts wryly. "I'm gonna be a dad before you are."

"I don't wanna be like dad." I glance over. "Or like you."

He grimaces, and it's a full minute before he speaks again. "You won't be. Because I'm gonna kick your ass to high heaven if you are."

I snort. But his words don't offer the intended comfort. And what about Macey? How do you go about prying nails out of coffins?

I must have mumbled that aloud because Jason chuckles. "Groveling's usually a good place to start."

Chapter Thirty-Six

*I*t takes several days before I'm ready to grovel. I have unfinished business at home that needs to be addressed first. It's weird pulling back onto the long drive that leads up to our estate. I have zero attachment to the place I grew up, no love for the ripening vines or the gently rolling hills. I don't think I ever have, but it took falling in love to figure it out. I still don't know where home is, but that decision is no longer up to just me.

I skid to a stop, because, why the hell not? I grab the briefcase full of spreadsheets from the passenger seat and step into the late August heat. It's blazing hot for nine a.m., and I fleetingly wonder if we're in danger of more fires this fall. We were lucky last year, but with the heat and ongoing drought, anything is possible. I don't remove my aviators when I step inside, and I don't wait for permission to enter Dad's office. He looks up, startled, then glowers disapprovingly. "Son?"

"Father."

"Aren't you supposed to be at your brother's?" he snaps. "And what the hell happened? You look like you've been in a bar fight. This is exactly why your trust fund has been frozen."

"About that, *Dad*. I've been doing a little digging while learning to make wine from my dear old brother. And I think you'll be surprised at what I've discovered." I make short work of the spreadsheets, outlining specifically how his board of ass-kissers has been fleecing him for years. He's ashen when I'm finished. "So here's how this is going to play out. You're going to release our trust funds. You're going to fire the board, then resign as CEO. You can remain chairman of the board, and I suggest you replace your outgoing board members with these people here." I add a folder to the pile of spreadsheets. "They've been thoroughly vetted." And include our former head grower Morrie, Marcel, and a number of the young winemakers I recently hired, including Isaiah. "Nico's agreed to be CEO, I will take over as CFO, and Dec will be in charge of acquisitions." Real estate's his thing anyway.

Dad's aged twenty years in as many minutes. He shakes his head slowly. "I don't know how this could have happened. This isn't what I wanted."

"What you don't tend, grows weeds. Just like in the vineyard." I pat myself on the back. That might be the wisest thing I've ever said.

At nine-thirty-six, I hit the road. I don't push it the way I did last time. This is my last drive in my baby, and I want to savor how she handles. I've lined up a buyer in Kansas City, and I'll be kissing her goodbye. I'm a family man now, or at least I hope to be. I'll miss the way she handles, but it's time. And I'm leaving her in good hands - turns out my old college rowing buddy Harrison Steele, the tech billionaire, collects cars. My Pagani will be right at home in her new garage.

This time, I slow long before the speed-limit signs tell

me to. My heart beats more erratically with each mile I draw closer. By the time I reach Prairie I'm going twenty-five in a car meant to go ten times that. I pull to a stop in front of the bungalow that holds my heart. My hands are sweaty on the leather steering wheel. She could say no. She could totally fucking say no. And then what would I do?

Move on, I guess. I feel sick even thinking about it. My stomach churns in agreement. I glance down at the black velvet boxes on the console. She wouldn't say no, would she? Not when I'm offering her the moon? I let out a slow breath. I need to get my mojo back, fast. I can't show up on her porch and act... *weak*. I'm Austin fucking Case for crying out loud. I'm king of the goddamned wine world. I grab the boxes and jam them in my coat pocket as I step out of the car. It's got to be at least 103, but I don't care. Suit jacket stays on.

My throat tightens as I cross the street. By the time I reach the shade of the porch, I can barely breathe. The door flies open just as I'm about to knock. Our eyes lock, and the words pile up at the back of my throat. I want to say everything, yet can't say anything for the stark beauty of her. Her hair is piled up in a messy bun, tendrils that beg to be wound around fingers frame her face. She's pale - her freckles stand out across her nose, but it's her eyes I watch most closely. Relief mixed with horror. Maybe there's hope for me here?

She reaches up, gingerly touching the bruises which have faded to a hideous color of purple and green. "You look like Mr. Blonde got hold of you."

I huff out a laugh at her reference. "You should see the other guy."

She gives me a withering glance. "I did."

I touch my jaw. "I look better than Nash, don't I?"

She pulls off my aviators, eyes going wide when she sees my matching shiners. "At least you have both ears."

We stare at each other, each drinking the other in. I clear my throat. "I'm sorry. I said horrible things."

"You weren't wrong," she rushes to assure me.

"I was out of line."

"I made Jason tell me everything." Her eyes are luminous pools, threatening to spill over. "Everything. I'm so sorry. I didn't know."

I take her hands in mine. "You have nothing to be sorry about. Please don't cry, Gorgeous. Jason, Nico, Dec and I, we're working things out. It's gonna take time - but we want to... be better, for our kids," I finish, stomach flopping with the admission.

It's a big task, but Jason and I both agree, we want our kids to grow up free of the baggage we've dragged around for so long. I kiss her fingers and she lifts her face, eyes locking with mine. For a fierce, awful moment, the last remnants of fear clutch at me. But I can't live my life without this woman, so I swallow it down and speak. "We can figure things out, too. If you want," I amend, because I'm still unsure.

A tear slips out of the corner of one eye. "I want," she says on a hiccup and hurls herself into my arms with surprising force, burying her head in my chest.

"Look at me, Macey." She raises her head. I'm dead. Shot through the heart by the soft, hopeful look on her face. "I don't deserve you," I start.

"Shh," she interrupts with a shake of her head. "Don't say that."

"I mean it. I'll work the rest of my life to deserve you, to... not be an asshole."

"I like *some* of your assholish tendencies." She gives me a watery smile. "Maybe don't lose all of them?"

"I'll lose whatever you tell me to. You call the shots."

"How about *we* call the shots?"

It will always be a push and pull with her, but I think we both thrive on that. I cup her face, and drop my mouth to hers. Something in me settles like a key fitting into the right lock. I feel her smile against me as she opens her mouth with a sweet sigh of satisfaction. This is home. *She* is home. I taste her greedily, like a man starved. And I am, for her. We part breathlessly.

"Well?" She asks, tongue slicking her lower lip.

Chapter Thirty-Seven

*T*hat's my cue. The words I've been rehearsing for days now, that have jammed up in my throat, tumble out. And I'm not afraid. "I love you Macey. I think I fell in love with you the first night we were together. You never stop surprising me or challenging me, and I love it. I love you. And I love your crazy, wild daughter, and if you'll both have me, I want to be your champion, your lover, your partner, your everything for the rest of our lives."

Her smile melts me. It's brighter than the reflection of the sun off my Pagani when it's freshly waxed. "I love you too, you overbearing, oversexed beast."

"Just so we're clear." I take her mouth again. And when we part, I confess something that's been on my mind since my brawl with Jason. "I don't know how to be a father. At least, not a good one. I mean, I've set up a trust for you, Sophie, and the baby, but I don't know-"

"Stop." She places her fingers against my lips. "Nobody knows how to do it. You just... do."

I slip my hand inside my suit jacket and pull out the ring box. "Marry me?"

Her eyes go round when I open the box. "That's... *enormous*." She looks from the ring, to me, and back to the ring again. "I mean, it's huge. Do you expect me to-"

"Tell me that the next time we're in bed? And, yes. I do," I finish with a smirk.

"I can't wear that while I'm working in the fields."

"As long as you wear it in bed while I'm devouring your sweet pussy, I'm okay."

"Perv." She lets me slip on the ring, and rewards me with a kiss.

"Just the way you like it," I tease. I hope she never gets tired of my pervy side. "I have something for Sophie, too. Is she at school?"

Macey's face clouds. "I..." she takes a big breath. "I decided to homeschool Sophie."

"Why is that?"

"After... after you left, I got to thinking. I grew up running around a vineyard, and it was the best thing ever. And I realized after helping with the harvest, that as much as I like being a somm, I like winemaking more. And I wanted the freedom to help my parents, or help Jason and Millie, or-or-or..." She takes a deeper breath and pins me with a look that arrows straight to my heart. "Or maybe start my own venture. With Marcel."

"Yeah?"

"Yeah," she says, eyes daring me to disagree. "So even if you're done with wine after this fall. I'm not." Her tone says I better get used to it.

I pull her into my arms, kissing her senseless all over again. "We have a lot to talk about. But first, Sophie."

We walk to the park, and I spy Sophie way up in her favorite tree, wearing her favorite glitter tutu and a crown. Jason is standing below arms crossed scowling up at her. "Soph, I told you not to climb so high."

I clap him on the shoulder. "She'll be fine."

He glances sideways at me. "You let her down, either of them, and I *will* chop your balls off."

"Noted."

Sophie sees me and waves. "Hi, Austin."

"Why don't you climb down? I have something for you."

"Is it a pony?"

"Better."

"Is it a *unicorn?*"

"Better."

Soph shakes her head emphatically. "Nothing's better than a unicorn."

She is a hell-child, headstrong and stubborn, but it bothers me less, now that I know I have a role to play in shaping her. And while she knows how to push my buttons, I want her to grow up and not take any shit. I cross my arms. "I'm going to take your mom back home now. You can see it when you get home from the park." It only takes two steps before she calls down. "Wait." She scrambles down in record time, jumping the last three feet.

I pull out the other box and squat, suddenly nervous. Like puke on your leather shoes nervous. Talking to Macey was easier, by far. I swallow, mouth dry as sand. "So remember when we talked about your dad?"

"And you said bad words?"

Behind me, Macey makes a disapproving noise. I glance back at her with a sheepish smile, and she rolls her eyes, motioning for me to continue. "Yes." I nod. "And I said bad words. But do you remember what else I said?"

Her face pinches, and my heart turns to liquid. She nods, biting her lower lip.

"That no one can ever take your daddy away? And that your daddy will always be in heaven?"

She nods again, perfect bow lips pulling into a frown.

"Would you like to have a second daddy? One on earth?" I might have a cardiac arrest my heart is beating so fast. My stomach flips upside down.

Her eyes dart to Macey, then to Jason, then back to me.

"What I'm trying to say, is... if you'll let me. I'd like to be your stand-in daddy. Your second dad. Here on earth." I give that a moment to sink in. I'm so dizzy I have to blink hard just to stay focused on her purple sparkly shoes. I raise my eyes, heart in my throat. "What do you think? Would you like that?"

I hear Macey hiccup.

A crow caws from the tree.

The cicadas start singing, drowning out the buzzing in my ears.

It feels like eons before she nods with a tentative smile. Relief floods my body in a rush of heat. "Here. I brought you something." I open the box. It's a freshwater pearl necklace studded with blue Swarovski crystals, the same color as her eyes. "I thought when you wear it, you could think of your dad in heaven, and me."

"Can I wear it?" she asks, shyly, looking to her mother for approval.

Macey joins us, misty-eyed. "Of course, sweetie. Let me help you."

"Did Austin give you that?" she points to the ring on Macey's left hand.

"He did. He asked me to marry him. Just like Uncle Jason and Millie, and Sterling and Emma got married."

Sophie bounces so excitedly, Macey can hardly secure the necklace. "Do I get to be the flower girl?"

Chapter Thirty-Eight

*ne year later…*

THE SUV LIMO SLOWLY WINDS its way up the dirt road, turning at the gate, now open, wrapped in garlands and tulle. I can't help but smile at the difference a year makes. Marcel's home has been razed and replaced with a Frank Lloyd Wright inspired architectural wonder of wood and glass, an extension of its surroundings. It took all winter, and double overtime, but the buildings were ready before fruit set. Macey and I still disagree about money, but she can't deny that my money makes shit happen.

Beyond the main house - *our home* - is a series of outbuildings. One for Marcel, another, slightly larger, for visitors, of which there've been many since we welcomed a son in April. Drexel Arthur Case, four months old today, a chubby, gurgling, laughing, curly-haired redhead, just like his big sister and mother. But I think he's inherited my chiseled jaw.

I wait for the driver to open the door, and step out. "Holy shit," I mutter. I hardly recognize the yard. Macey banned me from the house yesterday, kicking me out before the decorators and caterers arrived. An enormous tent has been erected where the tractors usually park. Inside, I can see parquet flooring, flowers and crystal. White jacketed attendants are hurrying back and forth from the guest house, where they've set up shop.

A floral arch has been set up at the edge of the vine-yard, overlooking the steep hills dropping into Sonoma. White chairs are beginning to fill up with guests. I slowly make my way across the lawn to where Jason and Millie, who's holding my niece Audrey, stand next Dec and Nico and their wives. I raise a hand in greeting. It hasn't been easy, this last year, setting things to rights, letting go of the past. But we're getting there. And the women we love seem to have made it a priority amongst themselves to see us fully reconciled.

Jason grabs a glass of bubbly - Dec's creation - from a passing server and offers it to me. "Congratulations."

I salute him and take a sip. I feel... content. I'm still not used to it, but every day the feeling of disbelief, the feeling I don't deserve this level of happiness, fades a little more.

"Are you ready?" asks Dec.

"Absofuckinglutely."

Today is a celebration of more than just our marriage. The wine Macey and I created in consultation with Marcel will be unveiled at dinner. We couldn't settle on a name for it, so we didn't enter it in a tasting this spring. We also had other, more important events going on. I want to name the wine after the estate - Mt. Veeder Estate Rosé. Macey thinks we should call it Mr. Pink. I disagree. Not everyone appreciates *Reservoir Dogs*, or finds it as funny as we do.

A short distance from the arch, a string quartet begins to play. Across the way, the wedding consultant holds up five fingers. Five minutes and my ladies walk down the aisle to where I wait. I check again for the vows I wrote. They're still there, secure in my inside pocket. I slip my hand into the outside pocket checking for Sophie's bracelet and Macey's wedding ring. She was serious about only wearing her engagement ring in the bedroom, and so I've designed a platinum and diamond wedding band that won't catch on anything while she's at work. I really don't care what she wears, but I do like to see the flash of ice on her finger when I'm going down on her. Or when her left hand strokes my cock.

The wedding planner holds up two fingers. I drain my glass and head to the arch as the quartet plays the opening strains to Vivaldi's Spring. It may be coming up on harvest time, but we're still in the spring of our love, and I don't plan for winter to come anytime soon. Sophie comes skipping down the aisle, tossing rose petals as she goes. The guests sigh collectively when she stops to kiss her brother, cooing happily on Macey's mother's lap. She comes to stand next to me and takes my hand. "Is today the day you become my daddy?" she whispers.

I almost lose my shit, but I'm determined not to choke up in front of this crew. I'll never hear the end of it. I sweep her up into my arms and kiss her forehead. "You can call me daddy whenever you like," I whisper back, nearly choking on my words when I catch sight of Macey standing at the back of the aisle, a vision in white sleeveless satin designed by Declan's wife. Her hair is caught up in a low loose bun, and I'm already planning how to unpin it when I slip her out of her dress. All I can say is there better not be any buttons running up the back, or the dress is toast.

Macey laces her fingers through mine as soon as she reaches me, and together we stand before the judge. The judge starts talking, but I don't hear. My entire universe has collapsed into Macey and Soph.

"Daddy." Sophie nudges me. "It's time to give me my bracelet. Just like we practiced."

"Right, right." I put her down and reach into my pocket, then drop to my knees. I take her hand and slip on the bracelet that matches the necklace I gave her a year ago. "Sophie, I promise to always be your dad. To help you remember your dad in heaven, and to be your dad here on earth. For as long as I live." My throat catches on the last part, because what if I die too soon? What if I get hit by a car tomorrow? Or get cancer? The weight of my promise punches me in the guts. "I love you, Sophie," I choke. I take a big breath and swallow hard. "I promise to do my best every day to be your best dad, okay?"

"I love you too, daddy," she says as she gives me a hug. I think my heart might explode.

Macey brushes away tears as I rise. "Damn you." She lightly smacks me with her bouquet. "We practiced."

"I love you too, Gorgeous." I step in, wrapping my arms around her and pulling her flush. I catch her eye just before I bend to give her a kiss. I don't care that we haven't spoken our vows yet. We'll get to them. We've done everything else backward to this point, why not this too? What matters is that we're together, doing life our way, with our family at our home. And what could be more right than that?

THE BEGINNING OF HAPPILY EVER AFTER

Bad Boy Billionaire Sneak Peek

There may be squatters.

Danny's voice rings in my head as I slowly make my way up the long drive through the vineyard to where the crushing barn stands. Judging from the fancy cars lining the road and spilling into the vine rows themselves, these are pretty fucking wealthy squatters. Even before I can see the building, I hear music thumping into the night air, the low bass reverberating in my chest. What the *fuck* is going on here? Not for the first time, I wonder if my man Danny's pulled a fast one.

As I come over the rise, I see cars crammed in the open area like sardines. Holy Christ, *there's valet parking.* A young man wearing a reflective vest and holding a light wand waves me over. "Good evening sir," he says with a hopeful smile. "Can I see your invitation?" I'm sure the kid has made bank tonight. There have to be at least three-hundred people here.

I cut the engine and push open the driver's side door.

"Sir?" the kid asks again, this time with a note of concern in his voice. "Can I see your invitation?"

I glare at him. Actually, I do more than glare. I pin him with a look so stern I'm pretty sure I've made him piss himself. "I don't need an invitation."

Golden light spills out of the raised garage doors as I stalk toward the building. I'll give them props for being well-organized, whoever *they* are. And the guests look like a Who's Who from the society rags my mother's always perusing, glittering in Valentino and Dior, and wearing heavily adorned Venetian masks. Definitely not the unwashed, pot-smoking tent-dwellers I'd envisioned chasing off this evening. I've never had to hire security for any of the properties I own, but that starts tomorrow. As does a call to an architect I know to rebuild the house that burned down in last year's fires. Once the house is constructed and the outbuildings repaired, I should have no problems flipping this little estate, and making a pretty penny in the process.

I might be a prince in wine royalty, but my interest lies more with the distillery Danny's setting up on the property I just swapped with him in Kansas City. At the moment, I think he got the better part of the deal.

"Invitation please," a bouncer-type intones as I reach the party.

I blink, ignoring him. The inside of the crushing barn has been transformed into what amounts to a Vegas night-club. Red silk fabric hangs from the rafters with scantily clad women undulating and twisting themselves in the strands. Scores of candles and twinkle lights create an air of mystery around the scene. What surprises me though, are the lingerie models in various states of undress, moving through the crowd as if it's perfectly normal to wear next to nothing to a party. In an abandoned crushing barn in the middle of Napa. They're beautiful. Otherworldly. More like models in an art studio than Victoria's Secret models. Not an ounce of tawdry to be seen. Whatever is going on here, there's bank changing hands, and that pisses me off even more.

"What the fuck is going on here?" I growl.

The bouncer crosses his arms, biceps bulging. "No entrance without an invitation," he says firmly, jaw set.

"Who's in charge here?" I bark.

"Who wants to know?" he barks back, widening his stance.

"The property owner."

If he's surprised, he doesn't show it. He pulls another big guy over, says something to him I can't hear over the music, and the guy disappears into the throng. I spend the next minute in a staring contest with the first guy, heat rising through my body by the end of the second. I do *not* have time for this shit. Or the patience. Not after the week I've had.

The crowd parts and a vision in gold and black glides toward me. For a moment I can't breathe. My lungs simply stop working. She's like a Klimt painting come to life, erotically styled in black and gold fabric so sheer it leaves nothing, yet everything to the imagination. I can see the swell of her breast, yet the folds obscure her nipples. The top is open to her belly button, which is pierced and adorned with a gem as glacial as her eyes. Darker lace covers her treasure and a skirt - if you can even call it that - of the same magical fabric falls away in a vee shape drawing the eye down to gold stiletto sandals.

My mouth turns to dust.

She moves with a grace, a purpose… and a confidence that demands complete attention from everyone around her. I'm rooted to the spot, fire sparking from each of my cells as if I'd just stuck a fork in a light socket. I burn. And for a brief second, I wonder if I'm having a stroke, or a heart attack, or if I've developed some kind of neurological disorder, because this is the second time in the span of a week I've felt like this. Not from the gentle sway of her hips or her perfect posture, or in the elegant lift of her hand, but in the way her eyes see into the deepest, darkest part of my soul. All my secrets, all my sins, my vices... Everything.

I'm being flayed open by glacier blue eyes, and the result is a reckless arousal, a longing - *a need* - coming from a place so deep inside me, I don't recognize it. Hell, I don't recognize myself, and yet every urge with her feels so... inevitable. As if we were destined for this moment, even though I'm not religious and I don't believe in anything but the luck you make. On a cosmic level, my reaction makes no sense. It's brash, this overwhelming desire that courses through me. Feckless. But I can't stop it. I don't want to. I want her, in the most elemental way that two humans can connect.

"Who are you?" I demand roughly, mostly because I'm knocked off my game.

Her eyes widen, then flare with a heat that goes straight to my groin. "Who are *you?*" she parries with an amused smile.

I go still. I *know* this voice. But the woman in front of me doesn't match the woman whose voice I know. *She's* demure. Gracious. Elegant. A gift meant to savor. And absolutely unattainable. Except for the eyes, the woman in front of me is her polar opposite - hot where she is cool, unbridled instead of composed, yang to her yin. Cleopatra to her Elsa. Her voice is husky and soft, and sends prickles of recognition skating across my skin. Her plump mouth looks achingly, mouth wateringly familiar. I know the taste of lips like that, and the memory of it nearly drops me to my knees.

"Who are you?" I ask again stepping forward. "Answer me."

The bouncers move to block me, but she raises a hand. "It's okay, gentleman. Come with me."

She smiles at me like she knows me. It *must* be her. There's no way it's anyone else. But the more I try to make sense of it, the more I think my head is going to explode. I can't shake the feeling that this scene feels like something out of a Bond movie, and I half wonder if I'm going to get iced by some high-rolling gangster.

All I wanted was a quiet night on my new property, and some space to think while I figure out how to work around my father's latest manipulation. Instead I walk into exactly the kind of party that has cost me my trust-fund. How long before people just start fucking openly? Already, I can see writhing bodies in darkened corners of the barn.

I'm gonna fucking rip Danny's balls off.

But that can wait until I get back to Kansas City, because I *will* be paying Danny a visit after this fiasco. In the meantime, I want to get to the bottom of the mystery woman in front of me, although with each passing second, the bells of recognition peal louder.

The crowd parts again as she moves through them like a boat through water. I follow mutely, scanning the faces for some clue. But they're all masked. And likely drunk, or high. I recognize the signature cufflinks of an investment banker I know, but he doesn't acknowledge me. So... whatever game is going on here, the players involved prefer to stay anonymous. How very interesting. It's not much to go on, but maybe I can use that tidbit of information to my advantage at some point.

I follow her across the building to a door on the far side, covered by two more bouncers. She slips through and beckons me to follow. I shut the door behind me, heart pounding erratically, and more than a little irritated she knows my property better than I do. The sounds of the party die to a muffled thump of the bass. I open my mouth to ask the first of my million questions, but she's already halfway down the stairs, stilettos clacking and echoing off the dimly lit stone walls. This must be the way to the wine cellar. I dimly recall Danny mentioning there might still be barrels down here.

Her footsteps slow as she reaches the bottom of the stairs and another door scrapes open. I hurry to catch up, unprepared for what greets me as I round the corner and follow her through the second door. Instead of a large empty room, not only are there barrels upon barrels, but there are piles of fabric, feather boas, shoes, and clothing tossed about like a tornado swept through. The cellar is in utter chaos. "What the fuck is going on here?"

Worry flickers through her dark fringed eyes, but just as quickly she flashes me a brilliant smile, then turns to root through a mound of clothing piled on a folding table. "I could ask the same of you," she calls over her shoulder, before turning around and handing me a gold embossed invitation printed on heavy, black cardstock. "Why are you crashing a private event?"

I've received enough invitations, I can tell this cost a small fortune to print, just by the feel. I glance down to read the elegant script.

ONE NIGHT ONLY
Luxurious Lingerie by Madame M
5TH Annual Trunk Show.
Your privacy will be scrupulously protected
Entrance by Invitation Only

My mind races as I tuck the invitation into the inside

pocket of my suit jacket. How do I play this? My mother's dragged me to more trunk shows than I care to count, and I've never seen a trunk show like this. This is more like an invitation to a debauchery-fest. "I assume you're Madame M?"

Her eyes flare again, and her mouth twitches. I can almost see her eyebrows rising behind her mask. "Does it matter?" she asks coyly.

I take a step forward. "Oh, yes. Very much." I'm close enough now, that I can see her pulse fluttering erratically in the hollow of her neck. I'm overcome with the urge to bite it. Lick it, taste it. Hear her moan for more, the way she did last time, even while she begged me not to leave a mark.

Her mouth drops open, and her tongue slicks her lower lip, breaths becoming shallow. She's playing a dangerous game, and she knows it. And this time, I'm going to win. I drop my gaze, following the vee of exposed skin to below her navel, and slowly back up. It's ten degrees cooler down here, but I'm hot under the collar, in part because her tits have hardened to tight bullets, pushing through the material like soldiers standing at attention. It would be so easy to brush the fabric aside, see the gooseflesh arise with the brush of a knuckle. "Why is that?" she asks on a breathy exhale.

I give her a wolfish smile. "For starters, you're trespassing on *my* property."

She pales as her eyes widen to saucers. She gives a little shake of her head. "Impossible."

I nod. "Very possible, my dear."

"But Danny…" she trails off, speaking more to herself than me.

A flash of hot jealousy spikes through me at the thought of the two of them together. "Never take the word of a man whose great-grandfather was a notorious gangster." I've known Danny for years, and I like him. But I don't trust him.

Her eyes jerk to mine. "How do you, how do you-"

"Know Danny?" I supply. "I think the more important question is how do *you* know Danny?"

"That's none of your business," she snaps, standing taller.

I step closer and brush a knuckle along her jaw. Goosebumps erupt across her exposed skin. "It's very much my business, because you and I have a connection, don't we?"

Her breath is coming in shallow puffs now, her pupils blown wide as I reach behind her head to loosen the gold ribbon that keeps her mask in place. The ribbon slides apart between my fingers, and for a moment I hold the mask in place, waiting for her next move. Will she beg me to stop? Will she push me away? I should have known she'd remain still as a statue, challenging me with those eyes that seem to be my undoing.

My breath catches as I remove the mask. Although I prefer her naturally platinum hair over the black Cleopatra wig, she's no less captivating. "Hello, Emmaline."

She holds my gaze with an almost defiant look that quickly melts into hunger. The air between us sizzles with attraction and the corner of her mouth tilts up with a rueful quirk. "Hello, Declan."

Download BAD BOY BILLIONAIRE now to read about Declan and Emmaline.

Playboy Billionaire Sneak Peek

"*I*'m sorry man, it looks like you're broke." My accountant, Brett drops his gaze, and picks at an invisible speck of dust on his desk. "Dead broke."

It takes a minute for the words to sink in before my head explodes. "What the fuck do you mean I'm *dead broke?*" All the blood has rushed up to my head, leaving my fingers and my feet numb. I flex both just to make sure I'm not having an out of body experience.

"I mean, before you signed the divorce papers, it looks like Veronica emptied every single one of your joint accounts."

I slam both my hands on the desk and lean forward. Brett flinches, but at least has the balls to meet my angry glare. "Then you better start figuring out a way to get it the fuck back," I growl, trying my best to keep my field of vision clear. "You're an accountant for chrissake."

"Who you pay to do your taxes, not babysit your millions," he snaps irritably.

I think back to dinner, to the stilted conversation between me and Brett and his wife, Maggie - the glances I caught them exchanging, the thinly veiled hints from Maggie that I've overstayed my welcome… a sick feeling comes over me. "How long have you known?"

The guilty grimace he makes gives it all away.

"How long have you known?" I repeat, anger simmering.

"Ah… ah… just a few days," he says quietly, face turning a ruddy shade of pink. "I-I wanted to be sure before I… just in case…" his voice trails off.

"Just in case *what*?" I grit, the picture becoming clearer with each moment that passes. "Just in case you could eke out a little bit more blood from the turnip? Just in case you could line your pockets just a little bit longer?" God how could I have been so naive? "Fuck, Brett, we were college roommates." But not friends. Clearly, not friends. Stupid me.

"It's not like that," he sputters.

"Oh? Then tell me, how is it?" I'm so sick of this. Of the fake friends, of the betrayal, of nothing seeming like it is. A dark voice sounds in my head. *Karma, Nico. Karma.* It's right, the voice. My house of cards has been slowly tumbling to the ground, starting with dad locking me and my brothers out of our trust fund, then Veronica kicking me out, and ultimately getting knocked up by Senator Fucking Whelan, Hollywood producer-turned-politician, then demanding a quickie divorce. I push down a cynical laugh. Ironic, that when money's involved, a five-year marriage takes only days to dissolve. And now this. She's well and truly screwed me. Hit me where I was most vulnerable. *Just like you did to Jason,* the voice points out. Times ten. Fucking karma, indeed. "Why the fuck have I been paying you, Brett? You were supposed to look out for shit like this."

His face is the color of a beet now. "I know, I know, it's just-"

"That you were more interested in taking my money than *actually working.*" I point out, seeing the situation clearly now, for the first time. "So all that talk about friendship, about your house being my house, about how we go way back- it was all bullshit wasn't it?"

His mouth opens then shuts.

I slam my hands on the desk and rise. "*Wasn't it?*" For once, I want one of these money-grubbing assholes to just fucking be honest with their motives.

Brett opens his hands. "I'm sorry, man. I really am."

Sure he is. I shake my head and push off from the desk, mind already spinning options for what's next like a Rolodex. "Tell Maggie I said thanks for the hospitality."

"Do you have another place lined up?" The fact that he doesn't even bother to disguise the eagerness in his voice, is like a nail in the coffin to our 'friendship'.

"Yeah, yeah." Like I would tell him otherwise, or worse, beg. I pause at the door, hand on the jam. "And Brett?"

"Yeah?"

"You're fired." I head down the hall, past the man cave, where I've been sleeping on the couch for the past seven weeks, past Maggie hiding in the kitchen, to the front hall where my backpack and leather jacket hang in the corner. I haven't worn the thing since college because Veronica hated it. So when she unceremoniously kicked me out, I took perverse pleasure in grabbing it from the closet, wheeling my Ducati out of the garage, and kicking up a rooster tail of gravel as I sped off.

There's no need for a dramatic exit here. I'm done, and I just want to move the fuck on. The cool salty dew of the marine layer hits my face as I slip out the front door.

Fitting, that it never cleared today. There won't be a riding off into the sunset moment for me, only disappearing into the fog. Also fitting.

I take one last look around the fancy Carmel Highlands neighborhood, with its gracious houses tucked between redwoods and rocky crags, overlooking the bay like tiny fiefdoms surveying their land. The whole reason Brett and his family live here is because of *me*. Gall burns the back of my throat. And how many others in the neighborhood are just like him? Siphoning money from the uber-wealthy to line their pockets, all in the name of *business?* The whole thing disgusts me. But what disgusts me more, is the unwitting role I played in all of it. Foolishly believing that my wealth secured loyalty, *friendship* to those I bestowed it upon.

I quickly check my phone. Weeks ago, when Veronica surprised me with divorce papers and let the tabloids inform me that she was pregnant again, this time with Senator Whelan's child, my brother Declan offered up his vineyard on Mt. Veeder. But I couldn't. At least not then. I'm the oldest of the three of us, and while it may only be by six minutes, I was the one groomed to lead, I'm the responsible one. And asking anyone for help, especially one of my brothers, would be admitting failure. But there's no use denying it anymore. I'm exactly that. Spectacularly. And it's either take my brother up on his offer, or camp on the beach.

I don't bother to text him to confirm I'm on my way. I already know it's unoccupied, except for a skeleton crew of day laborers working to rebuild the 1800's era farmhouse - I checked out the property weeks ago, just in case. I strap into my helmet and sling a leg over the bike, a part of me settling with the low purr of the engine beneath me. Tendrils of fog undulate and close in around me as I ride away - and the once billionaire prince, now fallen from his pedestal, is swallowed by the coming night.

―――――

THANKS TO FRIDAY NIGHT TRAFFIC, it's well after midnight when I roll to a stop, exhaustion pinching the space between my shoulder blades. I just fucking want to sleep. Okay, and drink. I could use a bottle of Scotch. Or bourbon. Or anything strong enough to make me pass out and forget the fucking mess I've made of my life. I cut the engine and gaze skyward. Declan scored big with this place, the air is clear and crisp, and even with the light pollution from Napa and Sonoma, and the city to the south, you can still see the stars. I didn't bother to ask him if it was planted, but you'd have to work hard to produce a shitty bottle of wine in conditions like this. The farmhouse, destroyed by fires a year ago, stands lonely and forlorn in the moonlight, lending a gothic feel to the place. To my right stands a double-wide trailer, most likely the foreman's office. Easy enough to crash there until morning when I can get my bearings.

I loop my helmet over the handlebars and hop off the bike, taking a moment to stretch before I approach the trailer. The tension across my shoulders relaxes a bit when the door quietly swings open. I flip a switch by the door and blink at the harsh overhead light. "Fancy digs," I mutter as I step into the room and drop my backpack. A desk with a laptop stands in the corner, but the rest of the space is... homey. A large leather sectional and a low modern coffee table take up most of the space. The kitchen is well equipped, and a round table with four chairs is nestled into the bay window. But what has my attention is the bottle of grappa and two small glasses at its center. It figures that Dec would have hired someone with wine knowledge. The apple doesn't fall far from the tree for any of us, even though we try.

I drop into a chair and pull over the bottle and a glass. I'd rather not drink alone- misery loves company. But beggars can't be choosers, and I need to drink away this day, this week, this summer from fucking hell. I pour a full glass and salute the empty space. "To karma," I murmur quietly, then down the contents in one swallow. The burn brings tears to my eyes, but I don't care. There will be time later to contemplate the finer points of this particular bottle, but right now, I want release. I pour another full glass and drain it.

The pleasant buzz hits after the fourth glass, and I let out a deep sigh. Exhaustion overtakes me, and I can barely lift my hand. I pour a final glass for good measure. This should allow me to sleep into next week, at least. And maybe when I wake up I'll realize it's all been some kind of a dark, twisted nightmare.

If only I was so lucky.

Nico

The first thing to hit me as I regain consciousness, is the constant stabbing just above my left eye. I groan and shift, only to be hit with the second realization - that my hands and feet are bound. I blink and wince, trying to sweep the grappa induced cobwebs from my mind. I try moving my hands and feet again. Definitely bound. My heart pounds heavily against my sternum. This is a nightmare, right? My subconscious is punishing me, right? I swallow and with extreme effort, focus my eyes, suddenly aware I'm not alone. I sit up with a mind-stabbing jolt. "What in the hell? Who are you?" I croak at the scantily clad and clearly furious creature in front of me.

"Who in the hell are *you*?" she bristles, holding some-thing head-level that takes me a minute to register as a cast-iron fry pan. "You drank my grappa," she accuses.

"So I did."

"You're trespassing."

I hold up my bound wrists, squinting, because it's too fucking bright in here. "So I am." Jesus, who in the hell is this woman? The foreman? With supreme effort I focus my eyes, and nearly choke on my own spit as the woman comes into focus. Never in my wildest dreams would I have expected to be tied up by a woman wearing some kind of big, fat rag curlers and a facial mask. The pale mask only serves to accentuate eyes so dark they're nearly black. And clearly pissed as hell. I swallow as my eyes drift lower. Scantily clad doesn't even begin to describe the sheer sleep-ing… thing she's wearing. So sheer, her dusky nipples and full, soft breasts call out to me like sirens. My breath catches somewhere in my chest. Her figure is lush, soft and curvy. The kind of body that begs to be squeezed and caressed. The kind of body you could lose yourself in, the kind of body that can take all of you. The polar opposite of Veronica. And God strike me dead for being a perv, but as I stare, my cock thickens, arousal pooling deep in my balls for the first time in months. Maybe even years.

"Hey. Eyes up here," she snaps.

Her voice pulls me out of my grappa-induced musings, and I make things ten times worse when I grin up at her. "Sorry, darlin'. It's not every day I'm held captive at my brother's place by a raving half-dressed lunatic in a facial mask and curlers."

She sucks in a surprised breath. "I am *not* a lunatic."

"So you do this kind of thing frequently then? Does Declan know you're here?"

"I'm calling the cops."

I lift my wrists again. "No need, sweetheart. Really. I swear I'm not going to hurt you."

"How do I know?"

"Well, for starters," I pull on the duct tape, my wrist nearly coming free. "I suggest you don't turn to a life of crime anytime soon. I could have busted out of your restraints five minutes ago."

Her eyes widen and she worries at her lower lip. "Why didn't you?"

I let out an empty laugh. "Because I'm too fucking tired, and my head hurts."

"Because you stole my grappa."

"Look, honey, if that's what's got your undies in a twist-" I drop my gaze to her hem, which is at eye level. "Are you even wearing undies?" I ask, my throat suddenly dry. She's not, and I can see the barest hint of plump pussylips flirting with the folds of her... whatever you call it. Fuck. It's the hottest thing I've seen since, ever. I shift uncomfortably, because in spite of the grappa, my cock is starving for something, anything besides my hand in the shower.

She lets out a squeak and lowers the pan, a dusky flush creeping across her chest. "I work for Declan," she grits indignantly. "But you still haven't told me who you are."

I drop my head- it takes too much effort to be upright at the moment, and I study her through half-lidded eyes. What kind of game is she playing here? She's looking at me like she knows me. *Really* knows me. But I swear I've never seen her before in my life. I don't recognize her voice, or her body. And I'm pretty sure, once the err... creative face covering is removed, I'm not going to recognize her face either. "I think you know who I am." I don't have the energy to be coy.

She lets out a sigh. "You're Nicholas Case, aren't you?"

"Nico." I raise my wrists again. "I'd shake your hand…" I shrug.

"Why are you here? Declan didn't mention anything about visitors."

The stabbing above my left eye starts again. "He invited me here weeks ago. Ask him." I crack open an eye, immediately drawn to dark buds puckered tight and pushing through the sheer fabric, teasing me with how untouchable they are. They might as well be eyeing me through a glass wall. I force myself back to neutral territory. "So you're the foreman? Very progressive of Dec."

She makes that squeaky noise deep in her throat again. "Hardly. I'm the winemaker."

That makes me sit up, albeit too fast, as my head angrily reminds me. "Wait. Dec's making wine?" Sonofagun. He's never shown the faintest interest.

"No. *I'm* making wine. That's why he hired me. That's why-" She shakes her head. "Why'm I telling you this?"

I flash her a mischievous grin. "Because I'm the kind of guy women love to confide in." Not. *So* not. If anything, I was the kind of guy mothers forbid their daughters to date. But maybe I'm about to turn over a new leaf.

Download PLAYBOY BILLIONAIRE to read more about Nico and Alison.

Billionaire Boss Sneak Peek

*S*ome people call me a fixer. Others call me a dealmaker. Really, I'm just an asshole with a fuckton of money. And tonight I aim to throw Grover Clevelands around like they're candy, not discontinued notes.

My phone buzzes as I pull into the long square drive of the Nelson-Atkins Museum of Art, and drop my keys in the valet's hand. *You're late. We're waiting in Kirkwood Hall.*

"Is that a…" The young man's eyes go round as he stares at my convertible Lotus.

"It is, and no you can't take it for a spin." My cell phone buzzes again. *Are you coming?*

The only reason I let Muffy Templeton talk me into releasing my inaugural cask reserve at tonight's Picasso wing fundraiser for the Nelson-Atkins Museum of Art is because her mother was bosom friends with my great-grandmother. That, and her husband Robert has no problem losing part of his fortune every week at The Whiskey Den.

I smell Muffy before I see her, drenched in her signature lilac scented perfume and dripping in diamonds. "Darling. You must hurry. The guests will be arriving in less than thirty minutes."

I kiss her wrinkled cheek, biting back a sharp retort. Instead, I wink at her. "You worry too much. I promised I'd be here."

She pats my cheek like I'm her son. "It's a good thing you're so handsome, Danny Pendergast."

She's not wrong. My looks and my charm have taken me much farther than the Pendergast name, not that it means much anymore. My great-grandfather might have been the stuff of legends, but his legacy lives on only in the mystique of a bygone era.

Muffy takes my elbow, leading me into Kirkwood Hall, which has been transformed into something out of the twenties, complete with a bandstand in the corner with an old-fashioned microphone. "I found someone to help you for the first hour. Once the whiskey's out, I hope you'll stay and mingle."

I nod, hoping the 'help' isn't her fumble-fingered grandson like it was the last time I let myself get talked into helping Muffy with one of her garden parties. Or worse, the granddaughter she's been trying to set me up with for the past two years. Don't get me wrong, I've enjoyed more than my fair share of debs — eager young women bored with college frat-boys and looking for a real man. One who deals in orgasms and no-strings-attached fucks. And there will be plenty of pussy here tonight, but I've got bigger fish to fry this evening. Muffy has pulled out all the stops for this fundraiser, and fully half of tonight's attendees hail from every major city in the country. High stakes poker, even for a cause, is irresistible to those caught in its web. I should know, it's what brought my great-grandfather to his knees.

Tom Pendergast might have spent his last days under a cloud of shame, but the fact he did hard time only adds to his legendary mystique. All you have to do is stroll through the Crossroads and count the distilleries and bars with his name on them. Me? I choose to honor my great-grandfather in a more... apropos manner. Helping damsels in distress, not asking too many questions about where the cash for my exorbitant membership fees come from. Building relationships with influencers in both the underworld and the business world, because it's funny, how often the two seem to be one and the same. But as long as my money keeps rolling, I don't give a shit. And tonight, the Whiskey Den will be hopping. I've made sure the word has quietly gone out to a few key members that a private, high-stakes game will take place after midnight. So as much as I'd like a tryst in a darkened corner away from the security cameras, I need to bring my A-game.

But one look at my *help's* backside has me regretting the choice to leave the condoms by the bedside table. I don't know what to appreciate first, the arc of her spine that flares into wide hips, or the long red hair that cascades to the middle of her back in thick waves. It takes a second to register she's carrying two boxes of booze-filled flasks, Muffy's idea to send my whiskey home with every guest tonight. I curse, and hurry to take the boxes. "Here. Let me."

I step around her and slip my arms underneath hers. The electricity when we touch is instant. Fire races under my skin, heating my blood.

Her gaze meets mine with a hint of amusement. "I've got it, thanks."

She's not beautiful in the cover-model sense, but she's arresting, and utterly unforgettable. High cheekbones highlight sparkling amber eyes. Her mouth is full and wide —

the kind of mouth that men fantasize about wrapped around their cock — and it pulls into a smile I can't help but return. I gently take the boxes, regretting only that we're no longer touching. "I wouldn't be a gentleman if I let you carry those." I set first one, then the other on a pair of high-tops and begin pulling flasks.

She joins, me, removing flasks from the second box. "I appreciate your chivalry and all, but—"

"Lemme guess, you've got it?" I turn to face her, but the remaining words die in my mouth when I catch sight of the snake tattoo crawling up and around her right leg, bared thanks to the insanely high slit in her black glittery dress. My mouth goes dry as I take in the rest of her front side. She's tall, nearly my height in her stilettos, which makes her five-ten, maybe five-eleven in bare feet. Her tits are like sirens, full and lush under the fabric stretched tight across them. My neck heats as I force my eyes to hers, because holy fuck, this woman could make a living as a goddamned pinup girl.

"I was going to say, I don't need rescuing," she tosses back, still amused, and extends her hand. "Roxi."

I take hers, perversely pleased at the grip that's as strong as my own. This is no damsel in distress, and it's sexy as fuck. "Danny. I brought the booze."

Her smile grows, and she makes no move to loosen her hand. "Ahh. Mr. Whiskey."

"Sure. You can call me that." Every cliché come-on runs through my head. I clear my throat. "Why don't you set up the flasks, I'll grab the rest of the boxes."

"Already done." She points to the other tables near the entrance. "These are just the extras."

"I hope you'll let me buy you a drink later, for your troubles."

"No trouble at all, and maybe."

"You have to let me thank you some way," I offer, not wanting this to be the end of our interaction.

Her eyes smolder as we lock gazes again. In less time than it takes to inhale, I'm hard. Balls tight and aching with need. "I'm sure I can think of something," she answers with a slow grin before turning and gliding away, hips swaying like a snake charmer.

A hand lands on my shoulder. "You might want to put your tongue back in your mouth, pal," says the laughing voice of Harrison Steele low enough that no one else can hear. "I could see the sparks flying between you two from across the room."

I turn to shake his hand. Harrison is one of my oldest friends, and was one of my earliest investors. "I thought you had a date?" My implication is clear — hands off. And it's best to be clear with Harrison, because he considers pussy chasing a sport. And if it was, he'd have won all the Olympic medals. It's hard to blame him, he's got those irresistible All-American good looks — dark hair, blue eyes, and at least according to my bar manager Lisa, a cock that's legendary. Women eat him up like they do pints of Ben & Jerry's. Me? I'm more of an acquired taste — whiskey neat, with a healthy dose of cynicism.

He scowls. "Ditched me."

"No fucking way. Kansas City's most eligible bachelor is flying solo at the gala of the year?"

"Not solo." He winks. "You're going to be my wingman."

"Oh no." I shake my head, grimacing at the memory of the one time I was Harrison's wingman in college. The night did not end well. "I told you I'm never doing that again."

"Aww, c'mon." Harrison claps my shoulder. "How was

I supposed to know that Samantha's friend was dating the president of TKE?"

"Because these are the things you bother to find out when you push your friend into the arms of a strange woman." Thank god the guy was so wasted that when he took his shot, he swung wide, and I was able to drop him with a right hook to the jaw. "Besides, I promised Muffy I'd tend bar until the flasks were handed out."

Harrison rolls his eyes. "Always behind the scenes, pulling strings like a puppet-master. When are you going to let go and start enjoying life?"

I sidestep his question with one of my own. "Where's Stockton?"

"He refused to come tonight because his mother keeps trying to set him up with one of Muffy's granddaughters."

"Stockton's mother has been trying to marry him off since college."

"It's only gotten worse," Harrison states with a scowl. She's taken to 'dropping by the office' with a new girl each week."

"Sounds like you could use a drink," I say, moving to the makeshift bar and filling a tumbler of whiskey directly from the cask. I hand it to him. "Tom's Special Reserve."

He lifts his glass in a toast. "To snatching kisses and kissing snatch."

"Who is she?" I ask, suddenly suspicious. It's not like Harrison to be that crude.

"No one," he answers too sharply.

"Liar. Your eyebrow always twitches when you lie," I say pointing to the corner of his eye. "Whoever she is, she's got you tied up in knots."

Harrison's eyebrows knit together. "The only tying up going on will be happening later tonight."

"But not with Roxi. Just so we're clear," I growl

pouring myself a tumbler. It's not like me to stake a claim, but I've seen Harrison work. He loves the chase almost as much as winning the prize. And I don't know what happened when Roxi and I touched, but I've never felt electrocuted by a woman's touch before. Not like this.

"Roxi, huh? That her name?" Harrison's smile turns sly.

"Don't get any ideas. My love life's off limits."

He spreads is hands. "I just want to help."

"You want to help? Spread the word — discretely — about tonight's poker game."

Harrison quickly turns serious. "What's the buy in?"

"Fifty." He knows I mean thousand. "Limited to the first five. If we have ten, I'll do a second seating at one."

He nods. "See you at midnight?"

Download BILLIONAIRE BOSS to read more about Danny and Roxi.

Do you love sneak peeks, book recommendations, and freebie notices? Sign up for my newsletter at www.tslayne.com!!

Find me on Facebook! Come on over to my house- join my ladies only Facebook group - Tessa's House. And hang on to your hat- we might get a little rowdy in there ;)

Meet the Roughstock Riders

A brand new steamy contemporary romance series filled with rodeo hotties and the women that bring them to their knees…

He's an ex-con. She's the sweet virgin he can never have.

When disgraced bull rider Ty Sloane agreed to take a job as foreman at Falcon Ridge Ranch, he didn't count on having to share his job or his cabin with twenty-one-year-old rising star barrel racer Maybelle Johnson. She tests his patience by day and drives him to distraction by night, but she's off limits—too young and innocent for the likes of an ex-con like him.

As far as Maybelle is concerned, Ty Sloane can go jump in a lake. The cocky bull rider is a thorn in her side, both at the ranch and on the road. But he makes her feel things no man has ever made her feel, and as she learns about his past, she can't help but develop a soft spot for him.

When trouble finds Maybelle on the rodeo circuit, Ty puts it all on the line for the sweet young woman who's captured his heart, even though it may cost him his freedom.

Download RIDE HARD today!

Also by TS Layne

TS Writes Bad Boys & Billionaires

FORBIDDEN BILLIONAIRE

billionaire secret romance

BAD BOY BILLIONAIRE

billionaire secret identity

PLAYBOY BILLIONAIRE

billionaire secret identity second chance

BILLIONAIRE BOSS

billionaire secret identity workplace

WILD THANG

billionaire secret crush sports romance

PU$$Y MAGNET

billionaire workplace sports romance

O MAGNET

billionaire fake engagement sports romance

BABY MAGNET

Did you know I have an alter-ego? Under the pen name Tessa Layne I write Alpha Cowboys & Hot Heroes

HEART OF A COWBOY

family feud/fake engagement

HEART OF A REBEL

opposites attract/workplace

HEART OF A WRANGLER

second chance

HEART OF A HORSEMAN

star-crossed lovers/second chance

HEART OF A HERO

old flame/PTSD

HEART OF A BACHELOR

secret baby

HEART OF A BAD BOY

fake engagement

HEART OF A BULL RIDER

Doctor-patient/second chance

HEART OF A RANCHER

enemies to lovers

A HERO'S HONOR

single parent/workplace

A HERO'S HEART

frenemies to lovers

A HERO'S HAVEN

secret identity

A HERO'S HOME

opposites attract

RIDE HARD

virgin/workplace/opposites attract

RIDE ROUGH

secret identity/frenemies to lovers

RIDE FAST

Acknowledgments

First, can I just tell you HOW MUCH FUN I had writing an Alphahole? In FIRST PERSON?? Yeah- it was that much fun, and I can't wait to bring you Mr. White – Austin's brother Declan. His story is going to be hot, hot, hot!

Many thanks to the outstanding crew at Cellar Rat Wines in the Crossroads- you guys are the best and I couldn't have gotten the wine details right without you!

As always, big love to my girls and Mr. Cowboy, you mean the world to me –xoxo

If you've read this far and you enjoyed Forbidden Billionaire, please leave a review on your platform of choice. Reviews from happy readers not only make my day, they help raise the visibility of our books.
   xoxo- TS